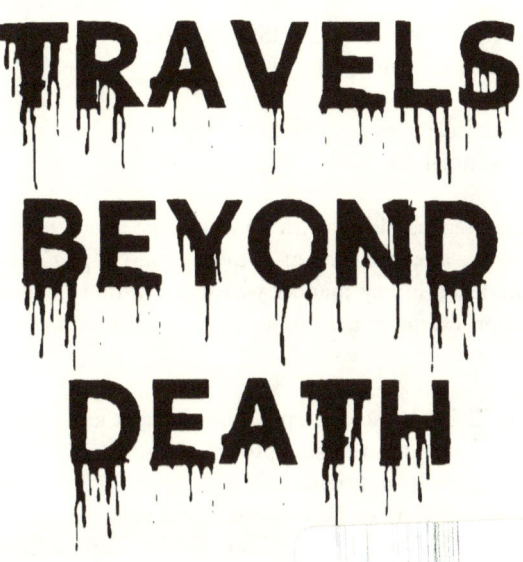

Dipavali Sen

Chennai • Bangalore

CLEVER FOX PUBLISHING
Chennai, India

Published by CLEVER FOX PUBLISHING 2023
Copyright © Dipavali Sen 2023

All Rights Reserved.
ISBN: 978-93-56484-59-7

This book has been published with all reasonable efforts taken to make the material error-free after the consent of the author. No part of this book shall be used, reproduced in any manner whatsoever without written permission from the author, except in the case of brief quotations embodied in critical articles and reviews.

The Author of this book is solely responsible and liable for its content including but not limited to the views, representations, descriptions, statements, information, opinions and references ["Content"]. The Content of this book shall not constitute or be construed or deemed to reflect the opinion or expression of the Publisher or Editor. Neither the Publisher nor Editor endorse or approve the Content of this book or guarantee the reliability, accuracy or completeness of the Content published herein and do not make any representations or warranties of any kind, express or implied, including but not limited to the implied warranties of merchantability, fitness for a particular purpose. The Publisher and Editor shall not be liable whatsoever for any errors, omissions, whether such errors or omissions result from negligence, accident, or any other cause or claims for loss or damages of any kind, including without limitation, indirect or consequential loss or damage arising out of use, inability to use, or about the reliability, accuracy or sufficiency of the information contained in this book.

Contents

Dedication .... *v*
Acknowledgement .... *vi*

1. Prologue - From the Bed of Metal 1
2. Kolkata 3
3. Wanderings 18
4. East Delhi 20
5. The Morgue 45
6. Again Kolkata and again East Delhi 48
7. Again in the Morgue 75
8. At Rajpur 77
9. Wandering Nowhere 134
10. Bangkok 136
11. East Delhi Again 151
12. Tihar Years 163
13. Tihar to Alwar 186
14. Delhi Again 206
15. Epilogue – From the Bed of Water 210

Contents

Dedication v
Acknowledgement vi

1. Prologue - From the Bed of Metal 1
2. Kolkata 3
3. Wanderings 18
4. East Delhi 20
5. The Morgue 45
6. Again Kolkata and again East Delhi 48
7. Again in the Morgue 75
8. At Rajpur 77
9. Wandering Nowhere 134
10. Bangkok 136
11. East Delhi Again 151
12. Tihar Years 163
13. Tihar to Alwar 186
14. Delhi Again 206
15. Epilogue – From the Bed of Water 210

PROLOGUE - FROM THE BED OF METAL

*I*t was icy cold on the metal bed with only a cloth to cover her. A strange smell hung about the room and a wisp of vapour formed above her. Where was she? She had never been in any place like this. Kushi wondered how she came to be lying here. Hadn't it been rough ground below her, with bristly grass pricking her? And before that, a polyester car-seat upon which she had leaned? She tried to remember, to re-live.

Stepping out of the building that had been her home for almost a decade, she had not known where to go or how. Then she had been bounding across Delhi to somewhere in Rajasthan, yes, Neemrana. Then had come a drowsiness, broken by a sudden shock – fear – the smell of hair-oil – then nothing. With the rough ground below and the night sky above, the morning light led her to this cold basement,

The vapour above her grew thicker. It formed a cloud. Wisps of it escaped the cracked glass pane of the door. It had *murdaghar* written in red paint outside.

2

KOLKATA

*K*ushi had grown up in an old three-storied building in Kolkata, taken decades ago by her grandfather Pralayendra Gupta, whom she called Dadu. Her father Balayendra, Baba to her, worked in a small town in the district of Birbhum in West Bengal.

Kushi recalled the Kolkata house distinctly. The three-storied house, a rented one, was divided or partitioned by Masonite boards blocking its doors and windows between tenants. Beyond the boarded-up doors in their part of the house, Kushi could often hear voices and footfalls of next-door neighbours, rarely met.

There was a garage right beside the front door but her family did not have a car. It was rented out to someone who owned a taxi but did not have a parking place. The black-and-yellow Ambassador, usually behind the collapsible gate at night, seemed to Kushi like their own pet tiger guarding their house.

Downstairs, the front door opened on to a small room where Dadu or her grandfather received visitors who were not 'family'. He was a staunch Gandhian and had been in Alipore Jail in the 1942 movement. Local people still came to him for advice and recommendation letters.

On the wall behind his table and chair, there hung a large portrait of Abraham Lincoln, saying, 'As I would not be a slave so I would not be a master'. It was the first thing one saw as one entered. Kushi had been seeing it every time she did, even as a newborn from the Bhavanipur Nursing Home.

The room led beyond her grandfather's table to other ground-floor rooms, including a kitchen with earthen stoves rising out of the floor and the stairs to the first floor.

That was where Kushi lived! And travelled, from floor to floor, room to room.

The school was the other place she regularly travelled to and from. It was a fledgling school, opened about a decade ago, not one of the established schools of Kolkata. Being still in need of local patronage, the principal himself had requested her grandfather to enrol Kushi in it. The school was so close that it could be seen from the balcony of their house and did not need any crossing of roads for Kushi to be reached and brought back from, by an elderly couple in charge of a five-year-old. But why were they in charge?

That was because Kushi's father had refused to shift to Kolkata from Rajpur, the semi-rural place where he was a college teacher.

"I am a small-town man," he kept on saying to his ageing parents. "Kolkata is not the place for me."

"How so?" Kushi remembered her mother arguing. "Born and brought up in Kolkata, with degrees from Kolkata?"

But her father paid no heed. Kushi's mother had been born in Hooghli and educated in Bandel and Chinsura. She had a strong preference for Kolkata. But she had to shuttle between the two set-ups that both needed her, getting torn between small town and city. Although she did not rebel openly, she often cribbed.

Kushi thus had two worlds to grow up in.

School, however, made her a little nervous. Her heart went into a flutter every time she entered it. She had to remember her full name which then was Kaushiki Gupta. There were other concerns. What if some of the sums went wrong? What if she landed up in school without her pencil, rubber or sharpener? What if she needed to poop or pee or, worse still, if her *jangia* or cotton panty became untied? For, the horrible truth was that when she had joined school Kushi could neither tie them herself nor untie them if they got knotted up. Ma had always done it for her and now it was Tthamma, her grandmother. She developed a little prayer or chant that she recited to Tthamma every morning she left for school.

All the sums will come out right, won't they?

I have taken everything along, haven't I?

I won't pee or poop at school, will I?

My panty won't come open, will it?

Tthamma answered yes to the first two and only after those reassurances did Kushi step out for school.

Whenever Ma came to Kolkata, which was usually to nurse Tthamma, frail and frequently ill, she murmured against this ritual. "Her whole nature has changed after she started going to school here." She recounted an anecdote at Rajpur, when still going about in a perambulator, she had made neighbourhood children – bigger than her - drive her perambulator across an empty stretch towards a house that belonged to a great-aunt who lived there by herself. "She was smart, she was brave. She had leadership qualities. Where is that girl of mine?"

Ma felt that Kushi was being cooped up among tall buildings and old people when she could have wide stretches and people of her own generation around. The school, in spite of its playgrounds and an ever-increasing number of students, was making a cowering personality of her. But Ma never did anything about it. Kushi learnt with time to tie her own panty strings.

But she did not drop that line from her daily prayer before going to school.

In the initial years, as soon as she had come back from school, changed into her light home clothes and filled her little tummy, Kushi had a happy game to play by herself. The rough patches on the floor provided a vast canvas for her paintings – with water!

She would sit down on the floor with a small aluminium bowl of water and a thick paintbrush.

The house had floors of red cement, rough in patches where it had been repaired. The texture there was rough and, on those patches, she would paint free-hand with her brush, dipping it only in water. She filled the floor space with lines and curves to make a picture out of them. She loved drawing fishing boats with nets cast on the water below as indicated by long curves with fishes in between. She squatted and worked from left to right, moving on as she finished one panel, so to speak. As she proceeded to the right, the lines on the left would dry up. They would leave little trace as they had been made only with water. For instance, the fish caught in the net would vanish and she would shift to the left on her haunches and put them back into the picture. She would make up a story in her mind as to how it had happened – like a sea-monster eating them up but vomiting them up on finding that they were poisonous. By then the pictures she had been making on the right panel would dry up and she would have to jump back to the right. Well, that was the fun of it!

Rather than clamour to be taken to the playground nearby, she would sit for hours painting on the floor with water.

In senior classes at school, she was introduced to Victorian poetry and found that Keats had composed his own epitaph as 'Here lies one whose name was writ in water'. *Bauls* of Birbhum too never wrote down their songs which were pure poetry. They regarded them as written in water, transient like life, not meant to claim lasting fame.

But Kushi at five or six had no such thoughts. She just found it fun.

Tthamma thought she had an artist in her and as the word spread, Kushi found her various uncles and aunts gifting her with crayons, colour pencils and painting boxes. Kushi transited to them but, her own style of 'water-colour' remained her favourite. Then an aunt enthusiastically arranged art classes for her in the neighbourhood. Kushi was introduced to 'still life' – copying arrangements of fruits and flowers in decorative bowls and to 'Indian painting'- equally 'still' in the style of long ago. Kushi had no enthusiasm or excellence in either. It was revealed to her grandmother that she had no particular talent for art. By and by, Kushi was withdrawn from the art classes. However, by then it was too late for her to go back to her own individual form of art. The fun had gone out of it.

A thin, spare figure, bearded in grey, Dadu sometimes took Kushi out for walks in the evenings. Rather than hop, skip and jump, that was the way she exercised.

She remembered Rashbehari Avenue with shops displaying glass cases of *saris* draped around mannequins, tram tracks in the middle of the street and pavements with flowers and balloons selling on them. Dadu generally took her to a small sweet shop near Triangular Park. He also got her inexpensive toys from the footpaths such as mazes fashioned out of wire, and tiny Chinaware dolls.

Dadu also told her tales from Indian mythology and taught her some Sanskrit prayers which he wanted her to say every morning at sunrise. He held the degree of 'Kavyatirtha' in Sanskrit.

From time to time, she went to Rajpur with Ma.

"Going home?" Her school friends would say.

Kushi wondered a little. Was this where she stayed not home then? Because Baba stayed elsewhere, unlike the fathers of all of her friends? But she forgot those barbs as soon as she boarded the train from Howrah. One by one, the stations on the 'loop line' went by and Kushi was immediately caught up by their charm. Finally, there was the little railway station with a little over-bridge over its two tracks. Baba would be there on the platform, cycle-rickshaws crowding around as soon as the three of them –Ma, Baba and Kushi - got out of the station. For, they got very few fares in that small town. Kushi had some friends there –neighbourhood kids – Tapen and Lila. And there was Minnie Tthamma who also stayed at Rajpur in a cottage of her own. But the days would soon get over and she had to go back to Kolkata. When she told her Rajpur friends that she was feeling sad, they looked a little surprised and said, "But you are going home, aren't you?"

Where *was* her home?

Memories of Molu Kaka also came to Kushi now as she travelled into the past as a wisp of vapour.

Molu Kaka or Malayendra was her father's twin brother younger only by a few hours, but a whole foot taller and more sharp-featured. He had brown eyes and a smile that showed up his sharp canine teeth.

He had always been a bit unruly and had finally left home. Never made good. Was a constant worry to the family, as long as he bothered to keep in touch.

She had seen her father often look at old album pages where the two of them were framed with golden 'photo corners' and protected by transparent but patterned sheets. Molu Kaka did brilliantly in school and college but, unlike Baba, he never pursued higher education. He took up a job right after becoming a graduate, one that took him away from Kolkata. Her grandmother sighed every time he came up in conversation. Kushi at her knees saw her write postcards to him pressing for news. She would get one-liner replies like, "No news is good news." He never quite went out of touch. He did write and tell them that he had got married on his own, and had a son, and one fine day, after an absence of years, suddenly landed up at their Calcutta home with his beautiful young bride! Then as suddenly as he had come, he left.

Kushi had no direct recollections of that visit, or even of a subsequent one when Kaku and Kakima had turned up with their newborn – a son, named Papu. Her grandmother had pleaded with him to take up a job near Kolkata. Molu Kaka had brushed the idea aside, as Ma would say whenever she recounted the matter later. "Bolu doesn't stay near enough, and you Molu are always on the move. What are we two to do? Mother of two and I hardly hear the cry 'Ma!'"

Molu Kaka had apparently said, "Well, you have got Bou-didi." That was Kushi's mother.

One visit she did remember, though. Their last one. When Kushi had been about ten and her first cousin Papu, six.

Ever since he came, Papu had been after her things – things which were especially hers. She remembered angrily complaining to Ma one day, right when she was making *phulka luchi*s specially for Kakima who loved them but considered cooking a chore.

"Why should I have to give away my *Alice in Wonderland* to Papu? It's mine. It's my prize for topping the class last year. Besides, Papu can't even read whole sentences."

"I know," Ma had drawn Kushi close. "But I know you have it in you to give it up."

"But why do I have to give up what is mine? Why can't Papu give up what isn't even his?"

"Because you're older than Papu," Ma had replied. "Because he is your little cousin. Because he is here on a visit. Can't you give up this little thing for him?"

Kushi had heard this before! Again and again. Ever since Papu had come.

"Can't you give up this little thing for her – your cousin? Remember, he has only come here on a visit."

First, it was her room. Then it was her favourite doll. Then it was her sketch pen set.

Something or the other, every day...

Papu wanted everything. Or, rather, Papu wanted everything that was Kushi's.

"The room is okay," muttered Kushi to herself. "I'll get it back once he goes. The doll, well, I don't know why he wants it when he is playing all the time with my building blocks. Sketch-pens too. Well, I can get a new set even if he finishes these off... But why my *Alice in Wonderland*? It's a prize I got at school. It's got that written inside under the school seal. It's mine."

Ma, frying the *phulka*s, had looked tired and hassled.

"Why is it that you know how to make these and Kakima doesn't?" Kushi asked, forgetting her own complaint.

"Oh, people are different. She knows many things that I don't."

"Well then, why do *you* have to make them for her?"

"For the sake of peace in the family," wiping her beaded forehead, Ma had smiled. "She gets upset if she does not get what she wants. Besides, I am the *bado-bou*, the elder daughter-in-law of the household. I have to hold everybody together – oh, well, you won't understand."

Kushi hadn't.

She had walked off to the balcony and screamed.

"What have you done to my doll?"

Papu had been there. He had taken hold of Kushi's doll and applied Kakima's lipstick and eye shadow on it. The effect was horrendous.

Kushi had snatched her old darling from Papu who had instantly set up an ear-splitting howl.

Both Ma and Kakima had come rushing.

"Can't you give up this little thing for him – your cousin? Remember, he has only come here on a visit."

That had been Ma, starting off on her old track.

"Didi, it seems your daughter can't stand mine. Neither can you."

That had been Kakima.

"Of course not," Ma had begun to apologize. "How can you think such a thing!"

"It is you who is behind all this. You don't want us here. You want to be the only *bahu* of the household, whom everybody praises because she is such a good cook while I can't even make my *phulka*s rise. You run the show – take care of the parents-in-law. I stay far off- away from the household and get forgotten."

With her hand sticky with dough and ghee, Ma had shouted at Kushi.

"Didn't I ask you to give Papu all he wants? The doll – the pens – the book? For some peace in the family, is that too much to give?"

Kushi had let her doll fall and run away. "But I'm not going to give that brat my *Alice*," she had sobbed as she had gone to her room, grabbed hold of the book and ran downstairs to her grandfather. She had poured out her woes to him and said, "I'll keep this with you. Then Ma can't give it away to Papu. *You* won't ask me to let go of my *Alice*, will you, Dadu?"

"I will," Dadu had put a wrinkled hand on Kushi's head. "*Tannashtam yanna diyate …tena tyaktena bhunjithhah.*"

"That old Sanskrit. What does it mean anyway?"

"That which you hoard, rots away," Dadu had translated. "Give it away, and enjoy it thus…"

"Makes no sense to me. How can you enjoy something if you give it away?" Kushi had said sulkily, "You don't even have it!"

"Yes," Dadu nodded. "But the other person has it and is happy. You have that happiness with you." "I'd rather have my *Alice*," Kushi had hugged her book close.

At lunch, Ma and Kakima had not been talking at all, and Baba and Molu Kaku too had been very quiet. The *phulkas* had got quite-limp and cold but no one had pointed it out. As they were about to get to the sweets, Molu Kaku had spoken. "We are leaving by the weekend." "Happy?" Kakima had spewed out the words as Ma had begun to protest and Tthamma, to weep.

The next couple of days, there had been no fights. No one had said much. Molu Kaku and Kakima had mostly been out shopping at New Market. Papu had mostly been with them – choosing loads of toys for himself. They ate outside, at restaurants and friends' places. Kakima no longer wanted Ma's *phulkas*.

It was quiet in the house. Almost like it was before they had come and would be once they were gone. Kushi knew she would get back her room, if not her doll and her crayons. Papu would no longer take away her things. He would not demand and scream.

And her *Alice* was still with her. She had *not* given it to Papu and was not going to do so either. Not for the sake of any family peace or Sanskrit sayings. Ma had stopped asking her to. The doll was enough to have lost.

The last day before they actually left, Kushi had taken a peep into 'their' room – her room that had been given to them. Suitcases had stood packed. Carry-bags lay about, bursting with goodies.

On the floor, Papu had been sitting with Kushi's old doll and a big mug of water.

He had put the doll's head right into the mug and was rubbing its face - making a mess of the red and black he had put on it…

"You meanie!" Kushi rushed in and pulled the doll out. Water splattered on the floor.

"Isn't it enough that you're taking her away from me although you have your own toys? Isn't it enough that you have made her ugly as a demon? Do you have to drown her as well?"

Kushi shook Papu by the shoulders. With such a force that even her heart began to flutter.

She had expected a kick in her shins or some such show of fight. Or at least a deafening howl.

But Papu had just looked up at her with sad eyes.

"I was just trying to wash her and make her as she had been. As you want her to be. And I am **not** taking her with me. I have many toys back at home."

"Yes, see? You know that yourself. You still wanted to take her away – just to be mean to me. Like now you want my *Alice*. I bet if you had it, you would spill ink on its pages. Just to be nasty to me."

"No, Kushi Didi," Papu had whimpered.

"As if I don't know," Kushi had shouted. "Why else would you want my old doll and my prize book?"

"I just wanted something of yours with me when I am gone and alone," Papu had trembled in Kushi's grasp. "I can't take *you*!"

Suddenly Kushi had felt as though she could not breathe.

This, from Papu! Not envy or meanness, but simply love and a longing for her? A yearning to have something to remember her by?

She had let go of Papu and run off.

When she had come back, it was with *Alice* in her hands, her prize at school– with her name on the title page–the book that was her own like no other book was.

Papu had been still trying to clean the doll's face – wiping it with his little hanky.

He had stared as Kushi had handed the book to him.

"But you don't want to give it to me!" he had stuttered in surprise.

"I *didn't*," Kushi had smiled. "Now I do. Just grab it, you pest."

Kushi had run off with a hug.

"Must tell Dadu that I have just understood some Sanskrit. That you do not share festers within you."

It had felt nice and warm inside her heart –the place the book had been taking up.

Kushi had been too young to learn what exactly the aftermath had been. All she remembered was that she never saw Papu again, nor Molu Kaka nor Kakima. She had seen elders come to the house and the police get rung up. Tthamma had gone into loud laments. Dadu had taken to his Gita. Her parents, both of them, had been wiping their eyes. All the relatives in Kolkata had gathered around. Minnie Tthamma had come up from Rajpur and stayed for a week, soothing Tthamma down.

A few years later, more rumours came floating by – rumours that Molu Kaka had left the country and sailed for London, to open a restaurant there. He had maintained no contact and neither had Kaki. There had been some hush-hush about it, something unsavoury and unspoken. She remembered Minnie Tthamma inquiring about him sometimes, in fact, whenever she came, but never pressing the matter.

3

WANDERINGS

*F*rom her metal bed in the morgue, Kushi went back and forth, both in time and space.

She could recollect lying on the rough, sparse grass, staring at the night sky. Where had it been? Haryana? Rajasthan? She wafted back there from Kolkata.

Crickets had begun to chirp. An owl had begun to hoot. A lizard had run across her belly. Kushi did not move. In fact, she did not feel a thing. She was dead. Stiffened by *rigor mortis*.

Yes, she had been travelling. To Neemrana in a taxi, travelling alone as she had told the taxi driver. He had asked for a fare in thousands but she had known that she had that in her *jhola* from Tihar. She had jumped in, the *jhola* scattering its contents… It was hazy after that, increasingly so. She sensed speeding off along a smooth road – for long. Then stopping – then a lovely drowsiness – then a shock – shock more than fear – trying to catch hold of something – the smell of hair–oil… then a grab upon her hands– by whom? Only pain and fear after that. A feeling of being jerked out, evicted. Then utter darkness clearing gradually to this uncertain state.

Her spirit had been thrown out of her body – jerked out – and did not know where to go. But it was on a journey – travelling – *pra itah* or *pretah*. Sent away from here – but not quite there – as Dadu would have split the word commonly used for ghost.

Kushi was still travelling.

Uncharted and unknown territories lay ahead. She could go anywhere she wanted, but where *did* she want to go?

Not into the future. Not there! She went into the past – down the memory lane –along "the stream of consciousness," to use the term coined by psychologist William Jones, used by novelist Virginia Woolf, and Baba sometimes.

Kushi's thoughts took an un-chronological jump from her childhood in Kolkata and to East Delhi beyond the Yamuna, five years after her marriage.

4

EAST DELHI

*I*t was still dark at 4 a.m. on a February morning.

Rahul will soon be home from his tour, Kushi – Kaushiki Chaudhuri now – thought with a quickening of her heartbeat. Yes, after full five years of marriage, it still quickened at the prospect of Rahul's arrival. Kuto, her son, was fast asleep despite his resolution of being up till his Daddy arrived.

He had called her up from the airport on the smartphone and now she saw the pre-paid taxi draw up before their house.

She opened the door and ushered him in, still smelling of foreign lands. He knelt down on the *durrie* and she kissed the top of his head in their own gesture of homecoming.

She tried to get him something warm to drink but he wanted her to sit and watch him unzip the luggage. He spread its content all over the *durrie*, pointing the items out to her.

"That toy Stegosaurus – it is battery-operated. Watch it move!"

"Kuto will adore it," said Kushi.

"And look at this cardigan." Rahul spread a pink fluffy delight out. "Just the thing for you!"

He also took out a fantastically huge jigsaw puzzle that he had got. "For all of us to do together," he said. The cover of the packet showed that it was also on dinosaurs in a primitive forest with a comet hitting them.

"How did the seminar go?"

"Oh, my presentation was very well-received. I got some great feedback. As for seeing around London, I could not do much. It was raining most of the time and you know I hate going 'Splotch! Splotch!' in the rain. Anyway, I had been there just two months back. Here, put this in the fridge," he took out a mammoth pack of chocolates, "till Kuto gets up. And now get me a *chai*. A good, homemade cup of *elaichi* tea."

She got up to go but Rahul pulled her close and held her for a brief second. "Good to be back!"

She smelt it again, the smell that lingers for a brief time around those just back from foreign parts. She almost broke away from Rahul to busy herself in the kitchen. She filled the electric kettle and switched it on. As the tiny light in it began to glow, she clutched the kitchen-top to stop sinking into her memories.

Of Rahul a decade ago, holding her close and whispering, "I'll come back for you after I finish at Kanpur. Let me go now."

A chance at the IIT was a big thing for Kushi, with her Kolkata-Rajpur background.

She had let him go.

This is how it had begun.

He had come down from Kanpur on some project he had to do with inputs from the IIM here. They had met through common friends and had fallen in love within a week. Both of them.

"I will write to you every week and make sure you do the same. The years will pass– I have only two years left, in any case."

Rahul had kept his word. He had kept in regular touch with her and come down to Kolkata (ostensibly to see his IIM co-partner, a little to his surprise because the project was long over).

As soon as he had graduated, he had got a placement in the fast-developing East Delhi beyond the Yamuna. He had not gone back upon his word. He had come back for her.

Kushi, by then, was also through her B. A. Hons course in a well-known but nearby college in Kolkata.

Dadu and Tthamma were no longer there. Baba and Ma had found nothing to object to the match, especially as they had known that their daughter had been waiting for him. Rahul's parents, in any case, had both passed away some time ago, when he was beginning his stint at Kanpur.

The wedding ceremony was a proper red-and-gold one, with all the Hindu rituals duly followed. Kushi loved taking the *saptapadi* with Rahul when she had gone around the sacrificial fire seven times offering *lajanjali* or oblations of puffed rice to it. "This is how we are going to go through life together – travel together through rough and smooth," Kushi had thought.

* * *

But when was the last time they had gone out together?

Early in their marriage, she had heard that Rahul was going to Neemrana to attend a day-long official seminar. She had asked to be taken along. She had heard so much about the hilltop fort turned into a hotel. But he had gone alone, and had come back duly impressed by the seminar venue. Those were the days at the earlier flat in East Delhi. Kuto was not even on the horizon. Rahul could easily have booked a weekend there later someday. But he never had.

And that other time in the first year of their marriage when Kushi had wanted to accompany him on a trip to Benares to offer *tarpan* for his deceased parents? He had joked. "Don't you know those lines of *Puratan Bhritya* by Tagore? *Patir puney satir punya, nahile kharach bade.* A wife earns her merits of pilgrimage through her husband; it gets too expensive otherwise."

He had taken her on an official picnic to Surajkund, though. She had loved it there, the steps encircling the *kund* of water that had once cured the skin disease of King Surajmal. When she had wanted to be taken there again for the crafts *mela* organized annually by the Haryana government, he had, however, commented: "*Gharer bou, gharey thakte bhalo lagena, na?* You are a housewife but you don't like staying at home, do you?"

Rahul's voice broke through her thoughts.

"Kushi, Kushi! Come and see. I forgot to tell you that I have got a kitchen timer for you!"

And she had forgotten that the kettle light had gone off.

Kuto was so thrilled with the Stegosaurus in the morning that he did not want to go to school but remained at home playing with it. Kushi got him ready and almost dragged him to the bus stop. She came back and rustled up some breakfast for groggy-eyed Rahul who had to attend office that very day. She gathered up the gifts Rahul had brought, tidied up the place a bit and then realized that her daily help Sita would probably not be turning up that day. "Beaten up too bad, I'm sure," she muttered and began doing the dishes herself. The floors she would leave for Sita to do tomorrow. But the clothes she decided to tackle by herself.

Sita had a wife-beater for her husband and often showed her welts and black eyes. "*Paer ki juti* – shoes on his feet – that is how he treats me."

Kushi felt for her.

But today she did make her appearance much later than her usual time, beaming, looking most cheerful. She had been taken to the zoo yesterday afternoon and was so tired after walking around it that she had overslept.

"But didn't you tell me only a couple of days back that he is a good-for-nothing, a rotter and a creep? That you don't want to be anywhere near him?"

Sita gurgled with laughter. "All that he is, Madam*ji*. But how could I say no when he came and said, '*Bahu*, let us go somewhere together.' 'Go by yourself,' I had said at first. 'Why ask me? I am not a jobless loafer like you. I have to do four households every day in a double shift.' But he said, 'What's the fun going alone to the zoo?' So, I... went along."

Would Rahul ever say to her about any place, "What's the fun going alone?"

In the afternoon Rahul rang up to say that he would not need dinner. He was taking out a businessman who might invest in their company. Kushi sighed. She decided to order a pizza – and Kuto was most happy.

Deepika WhatsApp-ed soon after.

She had just come back from Goa where her husband had a time-sharing arrangement with a resort. They went there every year for a week away from the work pressure in Delhi. Deepika went on about the beaches of Goa and how she had just had an anniversary-of-sorts there. Kushi and she had got married about the same time but Kushi had never even had a honeymoon.

Rahul had just joined service at the time and whatever leave he had, he had exhausted in attending his own wedding in Kolkata.

Deepika had sent a number of WhatsApp photographs of Goa. But Kushi had only glanced at them. It was somehow painful to see Deepika and her husband in the backdrop of the sea and the sky. She had no such thing to send back.

Even as Rahul came in at night, she put in her proposal for visiting Aksharadham the next day. It was so vast a complex that it would be as good as a trip and so close by.

"Aksharadham?" snuggling close in bed, Rahul asked.

"Just like that. It will be an outing together. It's the weekend anyway. No office for you or school for Kuto."

"Oh, okay," said Rahul sleepily. "But let me sleep late tomorrow, Kushi. I am tired. Don't wake me up early."

The next morning, she got up as usual but let father and son sleep. Sita came and went, rushing through her usual chores. Kushi made some bread-*pakoda*s and folded them up in foil to keep them warm and soft. She filled the flask with hot soup. She laid out the clothes they would be wearing on their outing. She woke Kuto up, bathed and dressed him. But, when at around ten, she went to wake Rahul up, she did not have the heart to. He was sleeping with such a beatific expression upon his face, sleeping so peacefully, so absolutely. No one could poke and prod and penetrate the realm he was travelling in.

When it was mid-day, she and Kuto had a little picnic on the balcony with bread *pakoda*s and soup. The other flats and the traffic shaded by the potted plants provided the setting.

Rahul slept till afternoon, and then woke up with a cry of "I'm famished!" He hung around her all evening as she prepared an early dinner, trying to help and getting in the way. "So good to be home!" he said more than once.

He slipped his feet into his old slippers. They were slightly torn and good enough only at home. But Rahul found them most comfortable. One toe stuck out and he wiggled it happily.

It became cloudy towards the evening and grey shadows flitted across her balcony floor, softening the black-and-white of its marble squares. Housework being done, Kushi came to the balcony and looked up at the clouds. Will it rain or will the clouds move away? Where will they fly to? She remembered the *Meghadootam* her grandfather had often recited to her.

There a *yaksha*, banished to Earth, had tried to send a cloud as a messenger to his wife whom he had left behind. But why had he not, in the first place, asked Kuvera to curse them both together to Earth? Maybe the thought did not occur to him. Else, they could have been banished together and set up home on Earth! Surely the *yaksha*'s wife would have preferred it rather than just sitting and waiting for her husband in the crystal palaces of Alakapuri? From Sita to Draupadi, wives have always preferred to travel with their husbands, however rough the path, isn't it so? Even Lakshmi had come down as Rukmini when Vishnu had decided to incarnate himself as Krishna.

The ring of the doorbell cut through her reverie. It was Veena, a friend. Veena was tall, thin and severe-looking, usually in cotton clothes in ethnic print, a social activist working for child labourers. She had given up government service to work for an N.G.O. in East Delhi. She was often protesting at Jantar Mantar, courting arrest and submitting petitions to various courts —not just attending seminars. She lived by herself in a nearby apartment and had struck up a friendship with Kushi at the 'Sombari' weekly bazaar that most women in the area loved to attend.

Driving a green Maruti 800, she dropped in occasionally at their flat and usually gave a patient hearing to Kushi. But she also did some plain-speaking, as, for example, today. "Stop cribbing, Kushi. I have no patience with people like you. Why do you need Rahul to take you to places? You can go yourself. Let him sit at home and take care of Kuto."

"But…" Kushi looked around the kitchen helplessly.

Anticipating her, Veena lashed out, "Oh, come on. Surely Rahul can look after Kuto for a couple of days. Surely, they can survive on noodles and sandwiches, or home deliveries? Or go out themselves?"

"That's not the point, Veena," Kushi wanted to say. "I do want to go out and see places – travel – take holidays. But I don't want to do it alone. I want to do it with *him*. What's the fun doing it all by myself?" But that, she felt would be unfeeling. Veena had no husband or child to be left behind as she was condemned to go from factory to factory, workshop to workshop, all on her own or with her co-workers.

She changed the topic slightly by saying, "I wish I had magic shoes, like in the Ray film *Gupi Gaine Bhagha Baine*."

"Stop waiting for magic," said Veena. "D-I-Y. Do It Yourself."

The next day Kuto came from his school bursting with news of a trek the school was taking its students to.

"Mamma, Sunder is going and Kapil too. All the Ma'ams will be going too. You must let me go, Mamma."

Kushi felt a sudden pang of envy. To see the steep hillsides with nooks and crannies bursting out with flowers and ferns…How she herself would have loved it.

"Of course, you will go, Kuto. And I'll come along with you," she said lightly.

"Oh, no, Mamma!" laughed Kuto. "It's only kids who can go. And the Ma'ams. You are not a Ma'am. You're a Mamma," he chuckled at his own joke.

With Kuto out on his school trip, that night Kushi asked to be taken the next evening to the Crafts Bazaar at Pragati Maidan in Delhi. "It's not too far!"

At the time Rahul was deep within her and grunted out a yes. But the next evening, when he came back from his office, he just flung his briefcase away on the wicker sofa and flopped on to the *durrie* before the television set.

"All I want now is to lie like a log!"

"But—" Kushi, all ready to go out, almost screamed. "You had promised yesterday to take me to Pragati Maidan this evening."

"Not now, Kushi. I am absolutely fagged out."

"You are always fagged out when it comes to going out anywhere with me."

"That's not fair, is it? There is so much work pressure and so much politics over my promotion."

"Last month I had asked you to take Kuto and me to the Surajkund Crafts Fair, and you said it was too far away…Before that, it was the Tughlakabad Fort. You said you did not have the time."

"I didn't. Besides, the Tughlakabad Fort isn't all that great, you know. I can tell you that. Gwalior, Chittor, Amer… Tughlakabad Fort is not a patch on them. I have been to them all."

"Yes, I know you have. But what about me? You have been all over India, all over the world. Gone on tours from Bangkok to Bulgaria. From Macchu Pichhu to Mongolia. What about me? All the time at home. Sitting and waiting."

"Oh, come on. You are my *gharani, grihini*. Where else would you be?"

"Don't laugh it off," said Kushi, in tears by then. "Tell me, do you ever think of me while you are away, in all those exotic places?"

"Of course, I do! I wonder what you are doing and think how good it would be to get back home to you," Rahul's tone was soothing.

"Yes, but while on the trip…don't you ever want me beside you? Seeing things with you, doing things with you, sharing things with you?"

Rahul was silent and Kushi said, "See, you don't."

"What nonsense!" Rahul was indignant. "You know I can't take you along with me on every office trip."

"But on just a few? Besides, what about closer to home? Why can't you take me to Mumbai or Kolkata? Or Pragati Maidan or Tughlakabad Fort?"

"Kushi, what's got into you? Why go on like this when you see I am so tired?"

But Kushi went on. "You bring me perfumes and gadgets from abroad, and give me details of your trip. But you never say, 'Kushi, if only you had been there with me!' You just don't think of me when you are there."

"But I do. How else do you think I get all those gifts for you? When I buy them, I am thinking of you, am I not?"

"It's not the same thing as my being with you."

"Kushi, I just don't get you."

Kushi's eyes fell on the knick-knacks around the room. The bamboo lampshade from Tripura – a peacock in brown and ochre. The wooden Matrioskha dolls from Russia. The Swarowski bird from some airport or the other. The *batik* wall-hanging from Indonesia.

She felt a wild urge to swipe at them and knock them down, and stand among the broken bits. Rahul got up from the *durrie* and kissed her on the nape of her neck. "Cool down. Your favourite serial is about to start."

The next day Rahul rang up from the office in the afternoon. "I have to leave early tomorrow for Bombay. For a full week this time. Get my clothes collected from the laundry and pack a few things into my suitcase."

It was drizzling. Kushi rang up the laundry for home delivery. As Rahul was generally on the move, she had become an expert in gathering up his towels and tissues, shaving kit and digestives.

She took care to cook the meatballs just the way that Rahul liked them. For Kuto, she kept aside a less spicy *avatara*. The laundry was delivered, and when he came, rather late, Rahul was pleased to find everything in order for him.

It was cosy to be in and have home-cooked meatballs. Rahul looked happy. But after dinner, when Kushi was clearing the table, he suddenly yanked at her. "Come on, let's go out at once."

Kushi paused.

"Oh, forget about that table. Just let's go out."

"There's so much work left—"

"Forget it!"

"But Kuto, he has fallen asleep. We can't go out leaving him alone…"

"No, of course not. I'll carry him down to the car. You just hurry."

Kushi made a move towards the built-in cupboard where she kept her saris.

"Come on, hurry!" Rahul had already scooped Kuto up.

He was already at the door.

"I have to change, you know," Kushi shouted back. "I can't go out in this old thing."

"Oh, come on! How does it matter?" He added with a light compliment, "You are equally stunning in everything you wear!" He caressed her with his voice. "Just come."

What had got into him? Had she finally got through to him? Was he taking her out tonight? This wonderful night with its maddening smell of wet earth? Oh, alright, only for a brief spell before he left for the week. But here they were, going out together.

They laid Kuto – fast asleep – along the back seat of the car, and got into the front. Rahul drove somewhat slowly through the narrow lanes that widened into the circular Community Centre. Some of the shops on either side were already in darkness. Some were having their sheets rolled down with a crunching noise. There usually sat a cobbler along this corner, but he was gone. The flower vendor was winding up. The long sticks of Rajnigandha gleamed in their transparent sheets as Rahul drove past the lane.

They emerged on the main road – a wider strip of glistening black. A few cars passed by with their headlights lighting up the road for fleeting seconds. Kushi put her head out of the window and looked up at the moon with wispy clouds flitting across it. The air was like cold cream.

Kushi laid her head on Rahul's left shoulder. How wonderful it felt, even after years. She sighed with contentment.

But Rahul did not seem content to drive along the main road. Some way ahead, he turned again into a lane leading to a cluster of houses and shops. Again, most of the shops were already closed and a few were in the act. The juice stall stood in the dark. The popcorn vendor was pushing his cart away.

With her head still on Rahul's shoulder, Kushi felt him heave a sigh of relief, then inch the car forward and stop.

A little ahead there was a cobbler. He sat under a blue plastic sheet propped up by sticks held together with bricks on the pavement at the front and against the wall at the back. He was winding up but had not still done it.

Kushi moved her head away from Rahul's shoulder as she felt him bend down to take his shoes off. He straightened up and dangled them by the shoe-strings. Kushi stared stupidly.

"I had stumbled on my way upstairs. I hadn't noticed it then but at dinner, I suddenly saw ... this!" He pointed to where the right shoe was yawning open.

"My only pair! I had been putting off buying a new pair. And now, this catastrophe! All the shops are closed and I have that morning flight to catch. It's a bit of good luck to find this one!"

He seemed to pass the shoes on to Kushi. She took them almost unknowingly.

"Is that why we came out?" She got the words out.

"What else?"

"But – but – why did you bring me along? You could have come just come by yourself?" she asked, hoping that he would say something – at least something to the effect of *'I wanted you to be with me even for this little spell!'* Or, *'I thought it would be pleasant outside!'*

But Rahul's words were quite clear and otherwise. He pointed to the cobbler and instructed Kushi. "Ask him to stitch it up."

"But why – why do you need me? You can do it yourself? You could have come by yourself?"

"You have got your slippers on, haven't you?" replied Rahul impatiently. "You can walk up to the cobbler and hand the shoes over to him. Can I? My sandals are torn and I can't get my socks wet. I might catch a cold."

"You could take off your socks and walk barefoot?" The words – who spoke them?

"Ugh, no! The road surface is so rough and filthy, especially after the rain."

Kushi took the shoes and got down from the car. She took her steps carefully. For it was indeed wet and a bit slushy. One, two, three four... she counted as she moved towards the cobbler packing up. Five, six, seven... the *saptapadi* of marriage.

"And ask him to give them a shine after mending them," Rahul called out from the car.

"Madam, I will take it back to the car," said the cobbler. "It will take some time. Why do you stand here waiting?"

But Kushi shook her head. It suddenly felt better that way than to be together.

The next morning Rahul was gone very early, with his usual admonition of "Don't open the door to strangers. Be careful." It was accompanied by the usual embrace, but the words still sent a chill down Kushi's spine.

They reminded her of the experience she had soon after their marriage five years ago. Possibly the second or third time Rahul went out on a tour leaving her alone.

*

They were not there in this flat then, but in a much smaller D.D.A. flat, also in Jamnapar as the stretches beyond Yamuna were then called. The vermilion on Kushi's centre-parting was wider; the carvings on her white conch-shell bangles had no accumulation of dirt.

"Be careful. Don't open the door to anyone," her newly-acquired husband had said, standing on the threshold.

"Don't worry. I won't."

"Will you be alright? Are you sure?"

"Of course. Besides, I have to be. Since you have to go."

"I *can* cancel the tour... on the excuse of falling sick."

"And get colleagues laughing, boss displeased?"

Rahul went a few steps down their narrow staircase with betel-nut stains in the lower parts of the wall. His black bag hanging from his shoulder, his black hair shining. Then he came up again as Kushi stood at the doorway looking at him.

"Shut the door, will you? Don't stand there with the door gaping."

"Why, what could happen?" A note of irritation sounded in her voice. She wanted to wave at him again, at the bend of the staircase.

"This is Delhi, you know. You are new to it. You don't know its ways."

Kushi did have an idea. There could be petty criminals hanging around the block, keeping watch. The moment they saw that

Rahul was gone, they could materialize from somewhere, shove her aside and get into the flat.

Only last month it had happened in the next block. Robbery, rape and murder.

She had closed the door and latched herself in. What a fussy old man Rahul was turning out to be, she thought with a faint smile. In her mind, she could still hear his steps going down the stairs. Once she could hear them no more, it hit her that she was alone in the flat.

There was not much cooking to be done. The leftovers reposed in their small, new fridge. What about sorting out the carton of wedding gifts that still lay unopened? Most of the gifts had, of course, been sorted out earlier at Kolkata But some had travelled up here in a huge carton. Where should this Kashmiri book-rest go? Where should Kushi place this Tibetan wall-hanging? What about the books, sometimes received in triplicate? Some of the presents still had gift tags attached to them. Kushi could trace them to their donors. That spiky handwriting belonged to a friend of her mother's while this one was from one Amit ... a cousin of Rahul's, with a strong family resemblance in general build and even voice. She remembered him from the wedding reception. What about that one – was it from her school friend Mitra? Kushi squatted on the floor and pulled out one thing after another from the carton, piling them up on the floor instead.

There had been a knock at the door.

Kushi had realized with a start that it had grown quite dark. She got up and on the way to the door, pressed the switch for light.

But the room remained dark. It being October, the fan had been off anyway. She pressed the switch once more but even while doing that almost mechanical act, knew that it was load-shedding.

On this side of the Yamuna, unscheduled load-shedding was a common occurrence.

That is why there had been a knock rather than a doorbell.

The knock sounded again, more insistently. Automatically, Kushi responded with a "Coming!" Almost stumbling over the items scattered on the floor, she had thrown the door open. Silhouetted in the doorway, stood a figure that looked familiar. Amit, her husband's cousin. What a coincidence!

"Rahul in?" Even his voice was the same…No, not quite. Rahul's tone was usually serious. This one was a light, laughing tone.

"No, he's out. Actually, he's gone on a tour."

"So, you are not asking me in, is it?"

Responding unconsciously to the levity in his tone, she had said, "Why not! His better half is here, you know."

There was a pause and this time the voice was a shade more serious. "Not scared of your husband objecting?"

"I am not scared of Rahul – or anyone!" Kushi had answered in the same light tone.

"I see," Amit had stepped in and closed the door behind and they had been cast into the utter darkness of the room.

After a moment's awkwardness, Kushi said, "I'll get you something to sit on…"

"Don't bother. I know my way around. Been here before your time. Besides, I love sitting on the floor." He plonked down on the floor and immediately sprung up, hurting his behind on the edges of the knick-knacks.

"Sorry!" Kushi began to apologize to her guest.

"*Bhavi? Boudi?*" he said and there was a strange caress in his voice, "Relax."

Kushi had stumbled her way to the tiny kitchen and found a candle and a match box. She lit the candle, brought it and placed it on the floor in a corner of the room, afraid to place it on something that could catch fire. In candlelight, the room looked even more eerie. Amit sat at another corner of the floor, seeming quite at home.

Kushi ran her fingers through her hair and rearranged her *chunni*, even in the dark. She did not want to appear a domestic drudge before her brother-in-law, though he was a cousin close enough to have a family resemblance.

Amit began to chat, putting her at ease. He talked of the load-shedding, blaming it on the Delhi government's policy rather than the drought that was the root cause for insufficient hydraulic power generation. Kushi offered coffee but Amit said, "Cool it."

The conversation began to flow smoothly. Then he suddenly said, "Are you sure it is alright, this candle-light, closed-door conversation?"

"Amit Da," she said lightly. "This is not the Middle Ages."

"But in the Middle Ages all late-night conversation *was* candlelight, wasn't it?"

That made Kushi giggle.

"By the way, how did you recognize me so promptly? You had only seen me once and that too in the crowd of the reception."

Kushi explained how she had been sorting out the wedding gifts and just come upon the one that bore his gift-tag. That, and the resemblance she had noted, had somehow clicked at the same time.

"I get it." Amit laughed softly.

The feeble flame threw strange shadows on the wall. Street sounds floated up – bikes and cars roaring along the street, a neighbour singing *bhajan*.

"You certainly belong to this century...the young woman of modern times... not at all Rahul's type."

"What is his type, may I know?" Kushi did not like the sudden turn of the conversation.

"Well, you are his wife, don't you know?"

"We have been married for only a very short while," countered Kushi. "You are his cousin brother – roughly the same age – why don't you tell me what his type is?

"No. Instead, I'll quiz you, and find out how different you are from the girl of his dreams."

Kushi nodded, casting a moving shadow on the wall.

"Are you in favour of arranged marriages? Are they the right thing to go in for?"

"No."

"Why not?"

"It is such a risk – to go in not knowing what the other person is like. It's gambling, that too blindfolded."

"Second question. Are you in favour of pre-marital sex? I mean would you like to have a physical experience of the man you otherwise have interviewed and found suitable?"

"I wouldn't quite put it like that. But at least I would like to make sure that he is not HIV positive or impotent. Certificates would do."

"Wow! Third question. Forgetting about medical certificates, are you in favour of simply having a taste of it before the ceremony – I mean, finding out if the two jell together?"

"I don't think that is such a bad idea." "But supposing the prospective bride and groom do have such an experiment, and it doesn't work…Say, I apologize but have to put it like this, say, the fit is too tight for comfort, what happens to both of them? I mean the next ones they experiment with would not quite find them to be virgins. But forgive me, *bhavi*. I am going too far."

"No. It is a relevant question and I'll answer it for you. I, for one, do not hold to the ideal of virginity that cannot face reality. With the changing times, perfect purity is not possible or practicable. And let me ask you a question now. By the time a man marries, he gets ample chances of finding answers to the sort of questions you asked, whether through cronies or call-girls. How many women do?"

She heard the sharp intake of breath.

She went on, "Look here, I know what you are driving at. You want to know whether I was a virgin or not before I married your cousin. Isn't that it? Well, I have no problems answering that question as well. I was a pristine pure virgin and still it worked. There were no problems of fit, as you had put it."

"Perhaps you fit all sizes. Shall we try?"

The room was suddenly very quiet and dark. Kushi could not believe her ears. She felt for the first time that she was alone in the flat with a virtual stranger. The electricity was not back yet and the man she had let in was sprawled on the floor blocking the door.

"Well, what about it?" Amit asked in a mocking tone. Kushi felt her mouth go dry, and her heartbeat quicken.

"No!" she screamed but silently.

Amit stood up – a menacing figure in the flickering candlelight.

The walls showed arms outstretched and expanding like the claws of a demon.

She sidled towards the door – her legs shaking. Perhaps she could yank it open and get out? Then her eyes fell upon the brass candlestand. She bent to snatch it up. Her gown blew against it and the room went into total darkness.

She felt Amit close in upon her, put his hands upon her mouth and stop even the faint cry that was making its way out of it. She fought with all her might but Amit's arms were dragging her relentlessly down upon the floor.

She brought the candle-stand upon his face. The next moment the light came back.

She stared at Rahul as he raised a bloody face to her and got up – with herself held fast in his arms.

Later when he had been bandaged up and served coffee, Rahul explained.

"The flight was delayed for 24 hours. I was given the choice to wait it out at an airport hotel or to come back the next day. I couldn't resist coming home for the night. When the doorbell did not ring, or the staircase switches work, I knocked. Twice and then I heard you answer."

"But where is your bag?"

"I had already checked it in when the airlines discovered their problem. Anyway, as I was saying, you answered from within, and an idea came to me. Why not test you a little? You let me in, and it was clear that you had taken me for my cousin Amit. The devil got into me. I began to quiz you. I wanted to find out what sort of a woman you really are. Do you come up to my ideas of what a woman – a married woman – a good wife – should be? You see, I was so happy to be home for an unexpected day – to get a sort of bonus that I felt mischievous. Let me take you, through a test, to find out more about the woman I have married..."

"Well, what did you find out?"

"The answers were all wrong – they had me worried. I know we had met before our marriage and gone out together, and even waited for each other. But for you to have such views on the subject... well, it kind of unnerved me. With such views, how long could we pull along together? I went further ahead and tried to force myself on you. And then you gave me your answer – the right answer for a loyal wife to give. You passed the test. You are not just a good wife but a brave one– capable of defending herself." He gingerly touched the bandage on his nose and then said, surprised, "*Arrey.* you are crying!"

Kushi had tried in vain to hide the tears that had started falling some time ago.

"Come now, Kushi, don't cry. You passed the test, I tell you. I know now that I will be able to spend the rest of my life with you. You did *not* fail my test. Stop crying. Kushi, my Khushi."

Despite the endearment, Kushi took some time to stop. For, she had been crying – not because of the fear of failing the test but because of being tested at all.

Her husband had come to her as an imposter. She had accepted him as a fusspot, a chauvinist, a stuffed shirt, and never thought of putting him to any tests. But he had played a trick on her. Would *she* be able to spend the rest of her life with him?

Passionate though he was in bed, Rahul usually took precautions. He clutched Kushi like a child treasuring a toy, keeping it back in its box of thermocol packing.

He was waiting for a promotion. But that extra, unexpected night, he had taken none.

Soon Kuto was on the way.

5

THE MORGUE

*W*here are you now, Kuto? While your mother lies looking up at the skies paling at the approach of dawn? Going to your lectures – wherever they are? Dating a girl? Good luck, Kuto! No, no. I don't want you to get any idea of what has happened to me. Go your way, forge ahead. Let me lie on here, and get a few drops of dew rather than *Ganga-jal* from a *putra*. There are seven *swarga*s, the ancient scriptures say, and twenty-eight *naraka*s. Kushi wondered what her *swarga* would be like – the house in Kolkata, the garden at Rajpur, or the Temple of the Reclining Buddha in Bangkok? And her *naraka* –Pattaya?

Or perhaps this very room, the morgue?

Another body was being brought in. Duly placed on cold steel and covered in a white sheet, it was left there. 'Company for me!' It was almost a giggle that came out of the cloud above her. Soon she saw a cloud forming above the companion corpse. "Who are you?" Kushi sent wafts towards it. "I am a murder victim whom the police here have found. What about you?"

The answer came possibly in Rajasthani but Kushi could understand it. "I don't know. My son took me somewhere – far away from our village – and asked me to wait. He never came back."

From her voice, she seemed to be a very old woman. Kushi asked if she had tried to go back on her own.

"Where to?" she answered. "I don't remember. I don't remember anything nowadays. I could, till I turned eighty-five. But not now, not anymore."

Was she then a patient of Alzheimer's, or of Dementia? Become so much of a nuisance that her family had disposed of her in this way? Or had some accident happened to her son and prevented him from coming back to his mother?

"What happened then?"

"I just waited and waited and waited. How many days and nights I do not know. I called my son again and again till I forgot even his name. Then I just lay down by the road. I didn't beg but people still gave me leftover bits of chapatti and almost-empty plastic bottles of water. I wetted and dirtied myself on the roadside. And then yesterday or the day before, I had a pain in my chest that grew every second. I wanted to call my son again but I could not remember his name. I just lay there and a long, long time later, some men picked me up and brought me here. Who are they, do you know?"

Kushi did not know what to say. "Call upon Hari," she said in the end.

"That's it!" the old woman said. "That's my son's name. Hari! Where are you, Hari?"

It was all between two corpses. The call of a mother for her son becoming a chant for deliverance by Hari or Sri Vishnu. None could hear it but Kushi.

"Hari, O Hari!"

With that chanting of 'Harinam,' the vaporous entity that was Kushi wafted out again into the past. To her motherhood at Kolkata.

6

AGAIN KOLKATA AND AGAIN EAST DELHI

"Wherever your husband may be posted, and whatever the facilities his company may be offering, the first child has to be born at the girl's parental place," Ma had said.

Kuto, thus, was born in Kolkata at a reputed nursing home close by. Ma took over Kuto's care and that of her own baby as well. Kushi quickly regained any energy she may have lost in pregnancy and a C-section. So much so, that she accepted a sudden job offer down the street, at the tiny office of a 'little magazine' edited by a neighbour, Mr Chatterji. She had to supervise proof-reading while Mr Chatterji went looking for articles, ads and sponsorships. The baby reached its various landmarks of turning over on its back, sitting up and standing up. Its inoculations were duly done.

Rahul, meanwhile, had been making frequent tours to Kolkata.

On one of them, he said, "I believe we can now take care of him by ourselves."

Ma felt that it was too early still. "If he falls sick there – even if he develops a small temperature or upset stomach, Kushi will be at a loss to cope. Jamnapar is not all that well-developed and your job too is demanding. What about the times when you have to go on tours?"

A small tussle developed. Kuto took advantage of time ticking by and learned to toddle around on his own. He was one-and-a-half and even mouthing small words. On one of Rahul's visits, he had toddled up to him and said, "*Chai?*" Just the way he had heard it being offered to visitors.

That had done it. Rahul had insisted on proving to Kuto that he was no visitor. Ma had to give in. The neighbours too, it seemed, had started asking her if there was anything going wrong between her son-in-law and Kushi.

Mr Chatterji had simply said, "Well, it was bound to happen, but you were a good employee."

And so Kushi had given up her first and only job and flown back with her husband and son. Not only because that was the expected and usual pattern but because that was what she wanted. She had been missing Rahul and the home they had set up – beyond Kolkata on the banks of the Ganga, at Delhi on the banks of the Yamuna – Jamnapar.

Rahul had rented a new flat that was the envy of his peers and, looking around her new home, Kushi had said to herself, "This is my empire."

She decorated it as per her ideas. The kitchen was big and roomy, with a gas connection installed. She spread her *durrie*s on the sitting room floor even though it was now marble. She arranged furniture with the help of her maid Sita. She took care to put the delicate knick knacks out of Kuto's reach. She made the bedroom and the adjoining balcony pretty with potted plants. Even the two toilets were bright and fragrant.

Kuto was a love and it was fun growing up once more, as it were, with his toys, crayons and picture books. He was, Kushi noticed, particularly good with numbers. He did not fret for Kushi's parents but took to Rahul in a big way. Rahul too turned out to be a most affectionate and responsible 'family man'. Busy, of course, but duly available for any fevers or other small ailments that Kuto sometimes developed.

She also found a good friend in Veena though Rahul did not like her much. Kuto, however, liked his 'Masi' a lot. Never pandering him, she still had a way with him. Perhaps because she dealt with children in her area of work – child labour.

Kushi herself had had quite a different sort of childhood, but she had to bring Kuto up according to the time and setting he was in. Like several toddlers in their building complex, he too began to go to the playschool named Jack and Jill which was within the complex itself. Rahul sometimes dropped him there on the way to his office but naturally, it was Kushi who picked him up as he emerged in the afternoon from J&J, fiercely clutching his tiffin box and water bottle.

A while after she had set up a new 'home' in East Delhi, her old home in Kolkata had got dismantled with the death of her parents.

When her mother had first been taken ill, Kushi had wanted to go down to Kolkata for a week or so. But Rahul had squashed her wish with the words: "*Tumi gele randhbe ke?* Who is to do the cooking if you go off?"

Kushi had been so taken aback that she had not found words to retaliate.

Of course, when the news of her death had come, he had taken her to Kolkata and observed all the formalities with due grace.

A few months later, her father had had a fall and broken his left femur. Kushi had again wanted to rush to his side. "Let me fly – just for the weekend. I will prepare all the dishes. You just have to heat them."

"*Taka ekebare gachhe pholte dekhechho na?* You have seen money to grow on the tree, haven't you?"

By a terrible mischance, her father had never recovered from anaesthesia on the operation table. Rahul had been tender and comforting after that. And Kushi had blamed her bad luck for not being able to hasten to her father – even when he was no longer a small-town man.

As Kushi was an only child, and her uncle – Molu Kaka and his wife and child - had long been out of the picture, Kushi inherited all that her parents had. But it wasn't much, considering that the house they lived in – the house with the rough red floor– had been a rented one. Rahul had taken care of the legalities through a power of attorney from Kushi. Minnie Tthamma's house in Rajpur – which she had left to Baba in her will – was what Kushi had really come to inherit.

She found that she had a somewhat unusual neighbour downstairs.

Ms Dikshit.

The elderly landlord had told them about her when he was letting out his flat to them.

"Never any trouble. Permanent teaching job. So rent on the dot. Model of cleanliness, no complaints about water or power shortages, broken fixtures or gadgets. Never returning late or blaring out music. Hardly any visitors and mail, as I learn from the watchman. Smile on her face whenever we run across, sweets at Vaishakhi and Diwali. Agreed to the slight rise that I made last year to the rent. Alone and about to retire, she will not occupy my flat forever and stop me from letting it out at a hiked rate. Well, ideal tenant and ideal neighbour to have. Just you see."

Rahul had found her not only ideal but very real, as she brought them steaming bowls of home-cooked dishes on some weekends. She was always dressed in pastel colours and never used make-up. And she did know how to entertain small Kuto.

Her eyes were pools of serenity. But once when returning very late from some ceremony, they had looked up to see their neighbour on her balcony almost falling out in what must be an attempt to see the full moon better. Another day Kushi had heard the yowling of a cat floating up. Or had it been the neighbour crying her heart out?

But the next day when Kushi saw her, she looked calm as ever.

Kushi began to make up stories in her head. Perhaps she was a young widow who did not quite dress according to the traditional Hindu ways but did not transgress them either. Perhaps she was about to be married – the date had been fixed – but her groom had had an accident the day before the ceremony. Perhaps he had been threatened or bribed to keep off her –by either his parents or hers. Or, perhaps, he had ditched her for another woman – with eyes full of fun rather than serenity.

One day Kushi had asked her point blank. "You live alone – don't you feel scared? Or lonely? I mean, at times?"

Her neighbour had just brought her a dish of stuffed capsicum with some mango chutney to go with it. She had placed it on the centre table and sat down for the coffee that Kushi had hurriedly offered her.

Her neighbour had taken a sip and looked out through the balcony –just above her own balcony downstairs. She had stared vacantly at the grounds of the complex, the gates, the busy street, pedestrians, people returning home with shopping bags, children tagging along, autorickshaws, scooters, cars, vans, mid-day sun glowing upon them all. Tears had started to roll down her cheeks and soon sobs had begun to shake her. Could someone usually so cool sob with such abandonment?

But then she had sipped her coffee again and Kushi, quite unnerved by then, never probed again.

She noticed that her neighbour went out of station every now and then - whenever there was a short break of a week or so, say, around Easter, Dussehra or Diwali.

The first few times, she said, she had gone on packaged tours. But she had found those conducted tours too streamlined, leaving no breathing space for individual tastes. She had started to plan tours for herself and chalk out paths of her own. "It's more fun this way," she said. The last time, she had taken a trip to Khajuraho and before that to Udaipur. Not to the famous tourist spots, not to expensive resorts, but to the outskirts, often staying with village locals. Till now there had been no unfortunate experiences, and she had returned refreshed every time. She loved giving Kushi detailed accounts of her travels, the people, the place, the cuisine, the dresses, the customs, the scenic beauty and the architecture.

She never bought back much of mementoes and took along most of the items she could need on a trip. In fact, she kept a small bag packed for the purpose so that she could make a quick trip on a windfall holiday. Plastic ropes and clothes pegs, safety pins, foldable scissors. A non-stick pan, a spatula, a tiny stove and small packets of essential groceries. An air-pillow, a bedsheet. One or two dresses, a headscarf and a thick shawl. "Wouldn't it be silly," she said, "to spend time and money on such stuff when having my breaks?"

Whenever she went out of town, she requested Kushi to receive and keep her courier or speed post mail. There were a few, all official ones.

Kushi politely assured her every time and asked her where she was off to. It was usually the hills. "Take me along," she sometimes said lightly.

From a skylight in the morgue, which was in the basement, Kushi could see the trunk of a tree overgrown with grass.

The grass beat upon the pane whenever the wind was high. As if it wanted to come in. Again and again.

Like Rakhi Didi.

※ ※ ※

She remembered how the doorbell would ring and she would open the door to find Rakhi Didi on the doorstep, a fashionable suitcase on wheels by her side. She would grin her broad, toothy grin, come in and make herself comfortable.

She always arrived like this, suddenly, unannounced, out of the blue. That was her style. And Kushi would soon forget about the minor inconveniences of an unexpected visit, upsetting her daily routine.

The daughter of a friend of her father, Rakhi Didi would be making her visits from Ranchi, where her husband was now located.

She would like to visit the shopping malls and beauty parlours of Delhi, the Delhi Zoo or even the Tughlabad Fort. Even in her early fifties, she would overflow with the joy of life so as to carry them all away. Rahul would not be glued to his laptop, Kuto would not touch his homework, and Kushi would keep aside whatever darning or de-cluttering she had been planning to do. They would enjoy the visit enormously. Then, when Rakhi Didi left a couple of days later – she never stayed long and left as suddenly as she came – they would tell her to come again, and soon. Both Rahul and Kushi knew that it was too much to ask Rakhi Didi to give prior intimation and see her glowing face darken. The next visit, whenever it was, would be as much of a hurricane tour. Take her last visit, for example.

Kushi had hunted out laundered bedsheets and pillowcases. This evening, as Rakhi Didi sat munching peanuts on the divan, with Kuto lolling against her, Kushi asked, "How is Giten Dada?"

"Oh, he is fine," she answered breezily. "BP under control."

She launched forth into an account of how her husband had once brought a set of cronies for dinner without even informing her. At a moment's notice, she had cooked *biriyani* for them. But they had been so gloriously drunk that they had thrown it all up over her exquisite tablecloth. They had gone to sleep right on the sitting room carpet. The next morning Rakhi had cooked them a gorgeous breakfast and sent them home. "Giten is very proud of this ability of mine to conjure up large repasts out of nothing. After all, a man must have the liberty to bring home friends to dinner whenever he had a mind to. That's part of the marriage deal. Not just cooking the dull, everyday stuff for the two – or three– of them."

She looked at Kushi sternly and said, "You don't have it, I know. You are such a lousy cook. Look at the dinner you gave us last night. Terrible. Rahul is such a nice fellow to tolerate it day after day. After seven years of marriage, you still haven't acquired the abilities of a home-maker."

She repeated her admonition even at the beauty parlour. "Look at yourself in the mirror. See how slovenly you are. I wonder how Rahul puts up with you. You must take better care of yourself. Take facials, manicures and pedicures oftener. Let me tell you this. Men don't want to come back to a slovenly-looking wife or take her out anywhere."

Rakhi supervised the cooking the next day, tipping Kushi on new ways of peeling the garlic, turmeric and onion, on new recipes and new ways of setting the table. "You should see my dining table, not cluttered like yours – with ketchup bottles and coffee mugs. And I also put a bowl of flowers as the centre-piece. It is an art, you know, making a home for your husband and child to come back to."

Rahul said 'Wow' when he saw the spread. "It's straight out of the old *Woman and Home* my mother once used to get." For a second, he had looked nostalgic.

"Do take my tips, Kushi. Even if you are not a good housekeeper, which you are not," Rakhi smiled charmingly, "you can pick it up."

Looking at her earnest face, Kushi could take no offence at such bossing.

One evening Rahul suggested eating out and on Rakhi's insistence, Kuto was taken along rather than left with Veena, as Kushi had wanted.

"I know of your friend, and she is most capable. But you can't let the child feel left out."

The restaurant, which was rather a grand place, suffered damages in terms of broken plates and stained mats, and Kushi could hardly relish the elaborate dishes they had ordered. Nevertheless, it was an evening they enjoyed, Kuto most certainly.

Rakhi gave Kushi various tips on childcare the next day when they took a taxi from the taxi-stand outside their apartment complex and went out shopping again. She helped Kushi choose the right toys and clothes for Kuto, paying for them herself. She also made Kushi buy some new, potted plants on wrought-iron hangers for the walls, in addition to the corners of the bedroom and the balcony. They certainly livened up the flat. "See? This is what I meant by the art of home-making. I am a home-maker. I have a knack for it. Take tips from me and you will be able to set up a lovely home," Rakhi said with great satisfaction.

There were calls on the smart phone to and from Ranchi.

"Take care!"

"Look after yourself!"

"Yes, I will say hello to them from you!"

Kushi's father had always been most fond of this daughter of this college friend. Kushi remembered attending Rakhi's wedding – the first one. She had been around ten then and Rakhi, around eighteen. The bridegroom had looked quiet and shy. But Rakhi had been her bright, assured self. However, before the year was out, Rakhi began to run over to her parental place every now and then. The arrival of a baby did not prevent an official divorce. Rakhi found herself a job as a receptionist in a clinic quite far from her parental place. She began staying at a working women's hostel close to it. The baby was left with her parents and Rakhi visited them on weekends.

Kushi's house happened to be closer to the clinic and Rakhi began to drop in more than before. The entire household grew to welcome her visits. Kushi was in her teens and she began to be given well-meant advice, taught how to pleat her *sari* properly, make the correct folds, taken out to food joints around the corner, and treated to food and drinks not usually available at home in those days. Momos and milkshakes, for instance.

Kushi confided to her a crush she was having even while at school. It was one-sided, she felt. Rakhi laughed away any sense of gloom over this. "I know that kid. His father is a common friend of our fathers. I have seen him play with soap in his plastic bathtub. Just some bubbles, Kushi."

Occasionally, they would be joined there by Rakhi's "friends" – young men she treated with easy familiarity. Madhav, Anit... They changed from time to time and Rakhi seemed unconcerned about that. She also mentioned her daughter occasionally – but more as one mentions a niece than a daughter. She bought toys and dresses for her sometimes, when going for visits to her parents. The daughter – named Tuktuki–became a school-going kid.

Rakhi's hair began to tinge early with grey.

"It's the life that she leads," said Kushi's mother who considered her "a fast type" but never called her so to her face. She knew that

Kushi's father would not like it. Besides, in her own way, she was quite fond of Rakhi. "I never feel that she is a guest. Look how she helped me in taking the grime off that old saucepan of mine. And she practically shoved me off the kitchen and cooked prawns for the entire family. *Gharowa abar ghurunya*. Homely yet always on the move."

And then Rakhi turned up one day with *sindoor* all over the centre-parting. "Looking even more colourful, Rakhi. Have you gone and got married!" Kushi's mother had joked.

"Yes, Aunty! Just a while ago."

The details of the stunning news were shared freely and happily.

Rakhi Didi had met Giten Dada some months back. He was a senior engineer in the industrial town of Burnpur, soon to retire and settle down at his ancestral one of Ranchi. Their decision had been made and the parents had been informed by phone call.

The gentleman was duly invited over. Everybody took to him at once though initially, it was often on the tip of Kushi's tongue to address him as Giten 'Kaka' rather than Dada.

Rakhi's visits to their house in Kolkata became somewhat infrequent after this. Meanwhile, Kushi too had her Board Exams, joined college, and soon after, met Rahul. She confided her feelings to Rakhi on one of her somewhat infrequent visits. Rakhi asked to meet Rahul at the local restaurant and gave Kushi her instant approval. That is why Rahul too is so fond of her, Kushi smiled to herself.

There had not been any resistance to her match from her parent's side, but if there had been any trepidation, they had been blown away by Rakhi's infectious cheering for the two of them.

Soon after Giten Dada's retirement, Rakhi had given up her job and become a full-time 'home-maker' as she preferred to call herself. Tuktuki had been shifted to a school in Ranchi.

She had invited them all to Ranchi persistently but Rahul had never found the time. Kushi could imagine it well, the 'Home, Sweet Home' whose maker Rakhi was.

Rakhi Didi's visit was going on fine till one morning she announced that it was over.

Kuto clutched at her while Rahul exclaimed, "So soon! We won't let you go."

Kushi too made her requests. But she knew that Rakhi would not listen. Once she had made up her mind, she never tarried – she knew that from experience. Sure enough, Rakhi had already packed her red suitcase and glossy handbag. Sometime last night or early this morning.

Rahul attempted a joke about Giten Dada making a secret overnight call to Rakhi Didi, saying that he was missing her just too much. Rakhi Didi laughed in a good-humoured way but added, "Well, I am not going to Ranchi just now. I want to see the Taj again. I read a report that it was getting darker – the marble was getting polluted by the smoke from the industrial plants growing up around Agra. I thought of seeing it for myself, after looking you up."

"Where will you put up?" Kushi asked.

"Oh, I have a friend there. Remember that Madhav? The lanky one who once or twice came to that restaurant in Kolkata? The doctor? He's practicing in Agra now, married and settled down there. Young wife, a doctor herself. Madhav has kept in touch and often asked me to visit. I'll do it this time."

"And then get back to Ranchi from there?"

"Let's see...Can even go up to Nainital or Haridwar from there – have friends there as well."

Kushi knew better than to press her to either stay or go back to her husband just now. She asked instead about how Rakhi Didi planned to get to Agra. Rahul said that he could arrange a trip through his travel agent, but that it would need at least a few hours.

"Don't fuss, you young things," said Rakhi Didi. "The taxi-stand just outside? There's a fellow there I have already talked to."
"When?"

"The day when we went out shopping. While you were unloading the potted plants and all."

"Let me talk to him," said Rahul.

"Don't fuss over me and go off to your office," said Rakhi, laughing but firm.

In the next couple of hours that she was there, Rakhi reminded Kushi about putting cucumber slices over her eyes as she had shown her to, and also to foam up the coffee the way she did it, with a dollop of cream in it. "Take proper care of your husband and child," she said sternly.

She tweaked Kuto's nose and went down, refusing help even over the luggage.

To Agra, to Nainital, to Ranikhet. Or to Kolkata, and only then perhaps to Giten getting drunk alone.

She would come back again, Kushi knew, without notice, out of the blue. Kushi would be inconvenienced but welcoming. She would once again listen in all docility to her advice on building up a home. She would submit to all her attempts at making a good housekeeper out of her, her lectures on childcare and her tips on beauty care. For, she knew that there still remained something nomadic in Rakhi. She had not been able to make a home for herself.

Still, for some time after the visit, Kushi had dolled herself up for Rahul's arrival times and brushed up her culinary skills. But her efforts had largely gone unnoticed and she had soon slipped back into her old ways.

"Just be yourself," Rahul had said when questioned. "I like you as you are."

Hadn't he?

From the cold metal bed, Kushi looked at the skylight. It was a blank oblong. The grasses no longer reached its glass pane. The wind had fallen.

There had also been the visit from Apratim, Kushi recollected.

No one else in the world had that particular way of saying 'Hi'. Kushi had recognized him as soon as he had called one day.

He was passing through Delhi on his way to somewhere in Africa and had collected Kushi's phone number from Kolkata.

"Couldn't leave without hearing your voice," said Apratim.

"Hello," she replied. "From Rahul and me. Come over some day?"

"Polite as ever, aren't you? No, I won't come over –some day–– as you put it. I'll come now."

Kushi's heart was beating so loudly that she could hardly hear herself say, "Let me give you directions then."

As he ended the call, Kushi quickly ran around the flat, straightening this and that, hiding what looked shabby and putting forward what looked bright as a showpiece. A smell of rice burning came from the kitchen. Kushi had completely forgotten about the rice that she had put on the boil. "I'll think of it later," she said, pumping a sandalwood spray all over the flat, and then running a comb through her hair which unfortunately was dripping with the coconut oil she had just rubbed in – before taking her bath which was due.

She was only fifteen when she had her first remembered encounter with Apratim Ray. She had been dressed in a puff-sleeve blouse and a full skirt that reached below her knees. He had looked her up and down and there had been a look in his eyes that Kushi had never seen in anyone's eyes so far – the look of a man looking at a woman – and finding her funny, odd and laughable.

He had a mop of curly hair, thick square-framed glasses, a thin triangular face and a twisted grin. He was in torn jeans and a bizarre T-shirt. Like Rakhi, he was the child of a close friend of her father's. The friends had been in touch but their kids – Apratim and Kushi –had never met since very early childhood. Uncle Pradeep recalled how Apratim, as an eight-year-old, had once carried one-year-old Kushi around in his arms.

"She's too plump now for me to try it now," Apratim had immediately responded with an uncalled-for-remark. It had hurt, especially as he laughingly added, "She does not seem to have shed much of her baby fat."

There had been a few successive visits between the two families, following the passing away of her grandparents. Perhaps there had been a certain lifting of the weight of ancestral influence for her father. Perhaps he had missed his brother afresh and wanted to reach out to an old friend if not a brother.

But to Kushi, those casual visits had been fraught with feelings she had never felt before. All of her awkward, burgeoning womanhood, which while her grandparents had lived, she had not been very conscious of, had burst out in those few visits.

On one, while the elders chatted among themselves, she had taken Apratim to her room to show him her favourite books – by Mills and Boons to Georgette Heyer. "Who is your favourite author?" she had asked. "Maugham, I think, *The Razor's Edge*, specifically. I am like Larry there."

But Kushi had not yet read *The Razor's Edge* or any other works of Somerset Maugham. He had then mentioned a book named

Lazarillo de Tormes published in Spain in 1554. Lazaro is a 'Picaro' or wandering rogue who lives by his wits and laughs at social hypocrisies. From it had evolved the term "Picaresque" for novels with heroes who were roving and iconoclastic, but ridiculing the establishment rather than revolting against it. "I am a Picaro," he had said.

All Kushi could come up with was *The Vagabond*, a poem by Robert Louis Stevenson which was in her English text. The conversation on books had not really taken off.

Kushi had then dropped something on the floor – probably the pen she was holding in her nervous fingers. Apratim had picked it up and she had said, "Thanks."

Pat had come the reply, "I would prefer a kiss."

No one had ever said such things to Kushi.

But the maid had entered with fried *pakora*s, and Apratim had fallen upon them and not even tried to suit actions to his words.

A few more visits and then had come the good news. Apratim had got admission to an undergraduate course at Ohio University, that too with a full scholarship. He was going, going, gone!

Uncle Pradeep too had been transferred. There had been one final meeting. "For old times' sake," as the parents had said. Apratim had been full of his plans and prospects, thrilled that he had got admission into such a prestigious place, but there had been one moment when he had almost casually dropped the words, "Hey, what about that kiss?"

Kushi had shaken her head violently and run away.

That had been that. There had not been any pale blue aerogramme with Par Avion on them. No communication except for the occasional season's greetings from Uncle Pradeep.

As the doorbell rang and he stepped in, Kushi saw that he still had that old, twisted, sarcastic grin on his face. There was not an extra ounce of flesh on him. He was as slim as ever, maybe a trifle more muscular, and in a T-shirt and jeans.

There were the usual enquiries about parents, jobs, spouses and children. Apratim showed one photograph after another of live-ins, Maria and Joanna. Kushi too showed her family photographs of Rahul, Kuto and herself in a happy embrace.

Apratim was cool as ever, the picture of self-possession. And why not, thought Kushi. Who knew better than her that it was entirely one-sided–this weakness or crush that had not quite died. Rakhi Didi had also told her so.

"So, you are all settled down...at Ohio?" she asked.

"What do you mean? Picaro and settled down?" He grinned the lopsided grin that Kushi remembered so well, and stood up. "I am off to Kenya tonight to try my luck there."

"Lunch is almost ready – have it at home with me," Kushi's voice was almost a whisper,

"Aw, don't be such a typical housewife. Spare me the *khana-khake-jana* stuff. Let's eat out. Surely there are food joints around."

"I have to fetch my son from his playschool. In half an hour."

"Come on. Don't tell me you have reduced yourself to a domestic drudge, subjugated yourself to chauvinist tyranny!"

His thin lips – even more twisted in a sarcastic smile – knifed through her. All she could do was smile, and she knew it was a stupid smile.

"And you know we have some unfinished business together," he said, his voice suddenly tender.

Kushi gathered up all her loyalty towards Rahul and said, her voice suddenly harsh, "Some things are best left unfinished."

"Alas! My teenage love has grown up. Ah, well," Apratim laughed, taking it quite lightly.

He had several helpings of the lunch that Kushi now set before him. Then he got up to go. Kushi did not stop him. It was getting to be time to fetch Kuto. At the door, Apratim paused and turned. "You must break out of it, Kushi. Strike out for your freedom."

"Freedom? From what?"

"This cooking and cleaning, washing and drying, waving off your husband when he goes to work and fetching your child from playschool... and I can't imagine what other chores you are bound down to."

"I am not – bound – as you put it. Nobody's got me bound."

"Nobody but you – yourself," Apratim grinned and waved as he trotted down the stairs.

"Have a good journey," she wished him, shutting her eyes against visions of Africa as she saw it. *Born Free* by Joy Adamson had been a 'rapid reader' at school and *Chander Pahad* by Bibhutibhushan Bandopadhyaya, a favourite adventure read. The recent film *The Mummy* she had loved almost as much as the old *Cleopatra*.

Stretches of sand, herds of giraffes, baobab trees and the pyramids. She could not help having a pang of envy at the thought of Apratim flying out through sunset clouds with whoever it was beside him.

"Say something," Apratim turned back at the landing in uncanny anticipation of what Kushi was thinking. "You know I would give anything to have you by my side on this flight."

"Travel safe, Picaro," was all she could say.

For some time, she sat looking down at her own wrists, turning her *shankha, pawla* and *loha* idly around. They were all in filigreed gold casings but 'imitation' ones of good quality.

Looking down at them, she suddenly remembered her college teacher Deepak Poddar whom she had gone to see soon after her wedding. He had been sitting in the staff room before his old desktop, surrounded by his research assistants – all of them young and pretty girls. It was rumoured that being young, pretty and a girl was an essential qualification for being his research assistant. He had a serious problem with his eyes and needed assistants to carry out his valuable work – work that had received a prestigious government grant.

"Who's this now?" He had said, peering at her as if through a dense fog.

"It's Kaushiki, Sir, from last year's batch," said one of the research associates.

"Is that so," the professor had pretended to make another scrutiny through his thick glasses. "But she is looking awful."

"Now, now, Dr Poddar," said another professor in the staff room. "You shouldn't say such things to the newly wed. Say how pretty she looks and give her your blessings. That's the standard thing we are supposed to do."

Ignoring him completely, Deepak Poddar grunted out, "Awful she looks in those symbols of bondage." He had pointed to her *sindoor, shankha, loha* and *pawla* – the auspicious marks of a married woman among the Bengalis.

"Dr Poddar! You shouldn't be saying such things. It's an ill omen," said his utterly shocked colleague while his assistants – more used to this sort of remarks – merely giggled. "Be as iconoclastic as you like in the papers you write, but don't say it to our students – our daughters, rather!"

To avert a clash between colleagues, Kushi asked, "Did you get the invitation card, Sir?"

Her parents had seen to it that a general invitation had been sent to the department she had graduated from with an Honour's degree. But perhaps Deepak Poddar – her favourite professor in spite of his odd ways – had deserved a personal request – which she had omitted to make. It was the other professor – thinking it to be a common question – who answered.

"Well, I had my niece's wedding on the same day, but, of course, you have my blessings. *Ma, tomar sinthir sindoor akshay howk. Shankha loha bajra howk.* Let your vermilion be ever-bright and your iron bangle strong as thunderbolt. But I have my next class now." With this he was gone, lecture notes in hand.

"To answer your question," Deepak Poddar said, "I don't remember. But frankly, even if I got it, I wouldn't have gone to it. I don't attend wedding ceremonies – anymore."

"Why, Sir?" asked one of his assistants, as if to provoke him. Sure enough, a tirade followed.

"Because I am against the whole idea. I don't believe in the institution of marriage. It's bondage for the woman, acquisition of property for the man. And even if I did accept its practical necessity, I can't stomach the way wedding ceremonies are celebrated in our country and our society. Revolting, ugly."

He turned directly at Kushi and said, "You had been a bright student who asked questions in class. That's why I remember you. But now... know what you look like now? A performing monkey decked up in her chains."

The assistants had sniggered and even Kushi had smiled.

It was common knowledge that Deepak Poddar had been divorced by his English wife and packed off from London to Kolkata.

But why did this come into her mind now? Kushi wondered. Was it because of what Apratim had said?

The last she had seen of the professor was a few years ago when he was delivering a lecture at the India International Centre. Even though it was far from Jamnapar, she had made it a point to attend it. The last few years had made him more bent but certainly not broken.

She went up to him after the lecture. After a bit of squinting and frowning, he recognized his old student.

"It was wonderful to hear you again, Sir," she said. "How are you?"

"I am perfectly fine, thank you, and I am glad to see you are, especially since you have taken off those white and red bangles on your wrists. The iron fetter on your left wrist however is still clinging to you, or the other way round."

Kushi was glad she had taken the *shankha* and *pawla* off and put them in her handbag before she entered the IIC. The *loha* she did not have the strength of mind to take off. Anyway, it was a bit tight already after the thin layer of fat she had put all over with Kuto's coming.

But trust the Professor to have noticed it despite his glaucoma. She remembered it being said that he had no glaucoma where women were concerned

Other people were thronging around the professor by now. But before he turned to them, he had pointedly looked at her *loha*, and said, "Live – learn–see the world –spread your wings. But first, get rid of that ugly thing."

Did Apratim too think her ugly in her wedded form?

She shook off such thoughts and went to fetch Kuto. She brought him home, listened to his prattle, fed him and put him on his nap. When Rahul returned, she told him about Apratim's visit. He gave a quick, careless laugh. "Oh, that fellow! Your first love? No, no, your second, counting the Rajpur one!"

That brought thoughts of Rajpur – good old Rajpur!

Rahul had left for his Bombay trip. With shoes and eyes shining, doing the last-minute check on his Aadhar card and ticket, and calling for a taxi.

"Take care. Look after yourselves," he said again and again. "Don't forget to close the doors, I'll message you after checking in. Bye, Kuto. Bye, Kushi."

Just then the neighbour downstairs came up to say that she would be going on yet another trip.

"Where to?"

"It's a longer trip this time, and perhaps further...Let me go and find out! I have taken V.R.S, you know. Have got my P.F. dues and I can go to the end of the world this time."

"Great," but Kushi could not help adding, "Are you sure that is a good idea? I mean, isn't it better to put that money into FDs?" Instead of blowing it up, she added to herself.

"All that later," her neighbour answered cheerily. "After I am back from, say Goa, Daman and Diu."

"Have you got a booking somewhere in Goa? You can leave me the address or phone number,"

"*Arey, na.* I will go to the Nizamuddin Railway Station. So many trains from there to Goa – I'll take one. As for the address, none as of now. Goa is full of places to stay in. I will go and find something."

The eyes were as placid as per Kushi's idea of a lagoon. Kushi knew she would come back with her face glowing and make her sit down and listen to every detail of her trip. She had done it so many times earlier. Re-living her vacation and already dreaming of the next one. As she went down the stairs, Kushi waved back. Then she went in thoughtfully and reached out for the smartphone. She made a call to Veena.

7

AGAIN IN THE MORGUE

*I*n the morgue, Kushi's body was lying inert on her steel bed, with another corpse for company. Her spirit wafted along – not knowing which way to go.

But then aren't we like that even in life? We walk – sometimes on our own chosen paths but mostly on paths already laid out for us. We proceed a little way but find out that it was the wrong one. What do we do then – even as a living, breathing person? Was Apratim any less of a *preta* as he wandered – restless – hiding his insecurities under a garb of over-smartness? And what about Rakhi or the neighbour downstairs? Had she been any better when she had gone to Rajpur and further?

The morgue door opened with a clang. Three men came in. Two were in police uniforms. The third was not. He broke down as soon as the cover was taken off the old woman. *"Maiya re! Tu yahan kaise chalee ayi?* (O mother! How did you land up here?)"

The identification being done, they went out. Two attendants came in a little later and wheeled the body away to be handed over to the one who was obviously the son. Kushi never would know her name but at least Hari had come for her.

By herself again, she turned her thoughts to Rajpur.

8

AT RAJPUR

*I*t was late afternoon a day later when Kushi got down at Rajpur.

With Rahul on his tour, Kushi had struck out to be on her own for a couple of days. She had called Veena up and asked her to come over and take charge of Kuto. Veena had been quite happy.

"You do need a break," she had said.

Kushi had taken a Howrah-bound train but got down at Asansol for a train on the 'loop line' that would take her to Rajpur. Earlier there had been a steam-powered train which Kushi remembered with affection. Now it was the usual diesel engine. But the journey along the this 'loop line' was itself a change.

Once out of the station gate, Kushi got on to one of the cycle-rickshaws lined up outside.

The small town, with its once-familiar scents and sounds, wrapped her up in a hug almost as soon as the rickshaw started to move. There was the old chemist's shop at the central crossing, and the clothes store next to it. The footpaths had vendors spreading their cheap plastic-ware on blue polythene sheets. Local people were moving to and fro, a number of them on bicycles. The old cinema hall–the wavy tin shed of the Food Corporation of India – the white-washed church of Xaverian missionaries.

Then the divide in the road where Kushi asked the rickshaw to take a right. To her grand-aunt's house.

Minnie Tthamma, the head mistress of a reputed girls' school in Chittagong, had moved here right before the Partition of India. In this obscure Bengal-Bihar border, at least then, land and living had been cheaper than in and around Calcutta.

As Kushi reached the house, the crickets in the hedge were singing. Caretaker Jalpa, a young Santhal, came running from an outhouse at the back. There were many tribals from Bihar serving in Rajpur.

"After years, Didi!" he grinned, taking down her luggage, light as it was, from the rickshaw. He kept up a flow of happy but surprised inquiries as Kushi went up 'Crunch-crunch' along its path of red gravel. She went up to the little balcony in front. Jalpa unlocked the door and carried the luggage in.

It was clean and Kushi saw that Jalpa had indeed been a good caretaker. In a few minutes, she heard the clanking of the bucket on cement and Jalpa brought her water drawn out from the well at the back. This was the system here, yet unchanged.

After her wash, Kushi changed into a gown that she had brought with her and had the tea Jalpa's newly-wed wife Jhumri had brought for her. Like most Santhals, she was a smiling creature and not one bit shy.

"Didi," Jhumri said, "tonight, it's only rice and *dal* but tomorrow I will get chicken and vegetables, milk and eggs for you. How long will you be staying, Didi?"

"The week," said Kushi. "At the most."

"Oh, Didi. Stay longer!"

A train went hurtling by in an open tunnel that ran along the east of the house. The earth piled up on either side when the tunnel was being dug and the line laid, had hardened into embankments. The trains looked like giant caterpillars furrowing their way. They ran up and down along it all day and night, resounding against the two banks through which they ran. But they could not be seen from the house unless one ran to the edge of the embankment, and looked down. Mostly, by the time one had rushed out on feeling its tremor on the ground, the train would have gone away – with only the tail-end showing. That was the thrill of it, Kushi had always thought.

It was getting dark. The crickets in the hedges were putting up quite an orchestra.

Kushi settled in for the night, but after asking Jalpa to inform Tapen.

"Didi, I'll go right now."

It was a single bed but of generous proportions, and old Burma teak, brought over by her great-aunt. There was one flaw in it, though. A scratch made by Kushi at the age of three or so. Running a finger along it, Kushi stretched herself and now, only now, switched her smart phone on.

There being no Wi-Fi, she put it on data usage.

A video call to Veena who put a finger to her lips showed Kuto happily asleep in Veena's own bed. Kushi did not speak but messaged her arrival news and a smiley. Then she fell asleep with the crickets singing into her ears.

***

The next morning, she was woken up by the gravel crunching as Tapen came to see her, as early as he could after getting Kushi's message through Jalpa.

They sat together on the raised ledge of the balcony outside. "Jalpa's been taking good care of your garden," remarked Tapen. "See that bed of Nasturtiums?"

It was his way of saying 'Hello', Kushi knew. Saying it with flowers.

"A surprise visit... after ages?" he said next. The morning sun showed up fine lines on his forehead. Other than that, he was the same, a stocky figure in a brown *kurta* and white *pajama*s. "I had run across him yesterday morning and he had not mentioned a thing."

"He didn't know. Nor did anyone else. You are the first I sent word to."

"Honoured," smiled Tapen. Was it sarcastically? The next moment he was making polite enquiries about her husband and son and life in the N.C.R. – which seemed so far off now. He also asked if there was anything about the house here that needed his attention or advice.

There was something wrong with the fans, and Tapen said he would get his own electrician sent. "List out what else needs repair. I will collect it in the evening."

Kushi walked him to the gate beside which stood a Jarul tree, her grand-aunt's favourite. She noticed a sinister-looking weed at its foot and pulled it out.

"Do come," she said. "We'll go for a walk along the railway lines just as we used to."

"Sure," said Tapen, after the slightest of pauses.

Then he mounted his bicycle and was gone.

A train could be heard, hurtling down invisibly. For a second, Kushi felt like running up to the other end of the garden and looking down at the rail line below.

When her grand-aunt built this house of hers, Rajpur had been even less developed. But she had not given in to the relatives and friends who had discouraged her.

It was small, sunny and airy, with furniture of wicker and teakwood kept dusted and polished by Jalpa's father who was then the gardener coming from a Santhal village nearby. He also began to tend to the general upkeep, sometimes bringing his young son to help him.

Alongside the furniture, there were vases for flowers and holders for cacti. There was a tin rack of books including textbooks from the school in Chittagong. Kushi had often seen her great-aunt running her fingers through them with a far-away look.

Kushi took the duster from Jhumri's hand and dusted the rack herself. She buried her nose in the yellowed pages with their wonderful smell of old times. There were the scribbles she had made as a child in the *Tales from Ancient Greece*! Her grand-aunt had certainly made her feel bad about it. Well, she had been a headmistress after all.

Bath now.

The Indian-style lavatory was spotless as ever. In her late years, her great-aunt had needed a wooden framework to serve as a commode seat. It was a folding one and now hung on an iron hook in the lavatory wall. Minnie Tthamma liked to have everything in its proper place.

From a white enamel mug bordered in deep blue, the well-water poured over her like an old friend's embrace.

She lunched on *alu-gobi*, *daal* and *chapati*s Jhumri made for her. A childhood friend from the place who was still around had sent in some *chutney* and *kheer* through her maid, saying that she would drop in later, another day. Dear Lila, but Kushi was thankful she was not coming today. Today she did not want visitors. Other than Tapen.

In the afternoon, she sat on the veranda warmed by the day's sun.

Tapen came – as he had said he would. He looked as if he had just taken a bath.

At Rajpur

Soon she was clambering up the slope, holding her *sari* a little high and huffing and puffing the tiniest bit.

On getting to the top, they sat down on the ground of red gravel and thorn bushes. Kushi drew in the clear air and the smell of soap.

"Do you still use Lifebuoy?"

"Saw no reason to change my brand of soap," he said as he brought out a pack of *bidi*s and a matchbox from his *pajama*-pockets.

"Still *bidi*s rather than cigarettes?"

The striking of a match and then inhalation and exhalation. No other answer.

"Have you thought about the repair work that has to be done? Best to do it while you are here," Kushi began telling Tapen about it. A distant sound getting louder… a tremor in the ground…

A train!

Through one end of the darkening track, a goods wagon was seen approaching. It did not stop but went past, dragging its long, clanking body. Soon it had vanished at the other end.

"It feels just the same!" exclaimed Kushi. "Remember how we used to run up as soon as we heard a train coming?"

Tapen looked younger as he grinned back, "I do," but added, "Well, we, who are here, don't have to *remember*. The trains are passing throughout the days and years."

Kushi remembered herself as a seven-year-old coming to visit Minnie Tthamma, and making friends with Tapen who was only a little older than her and lived a few houses down the line. His mother, whom Kushi called Mashima, sometimes dropped in to see Minnie Tthamma, bringing her son along. She also sent him up to play with Kushi when she was here. It became quite a game of theirs to run up the embankment whenever they could sense the faint tremor and sound of the approaching trains. It had been a most astounding discovery for Kushi, accustomed to Kolkata streets, to come upon trains hurtling down at her feet!

Now that the train had gone by, there was silence again. "I am back," said Kushi suddenly.

There was silence again.

Then Tapen asked, "Why?"

"Just felt cooped up there."

"With your husband going places?"

"Right guess."

"Your son?"

"With a friend for a couple of days—"

"At the end of which you will go back?"

"I wish I didn't have to." The tears that had been rising all this while began to fall.

She could see Tapen make a move as if to wipe her tears away. But she also saw him check himself.

The light faded. The bulb on the solitary electric pole on the embankment came alive. Kushi saw insects gather around its white enamel shade, whirring their wings.

"Now that you have had your cry, let's get back. My mother will be sitting up for me and your Jalpa and Jhumri will be wondering."

As she got up, he said, "I will come tomorrow…A little earlier, so that we have some more time. Aha, be careful."

Kushi had got her *sari* caught up in the brambles.

He did not come in but left off from the gate where he had parked his bicycle.

Jhumri served her dinner and sat on the floor and chatted.

"Thinking of Jamai Dada?" she asked.

For a moment, it did not make sense but then Kushi was stricken. Why was it that she had *not* been thinking of Jamai Dada, that is, Rahul? Or Kuto, for that matter? She had travelled – more in her thoughts than the actual distance. It was as though she had fallen down a hole, like Alice, into a wonderland.

Once she had finished eating, she quickly turned to her phone. She had another fleeting glimpse of Kuto at Veena's place, playing with a set of dinosaur toys that Kushi had packed in with his clothes.

Then she went to bed again, with crickets chirping on the Tagar or Pinwheel hedges bordering the house.

Sleep did not come easily though. She tossed and turned within the mosquito net that Jhumri had hung around the bed.

Her grand-aunt had been strikingly pretty. As a student of Bethune College, Calcutta, she had been known as her year's Bethune Beauty. She had heard her father and uncle tease her.

"Masi, that great scientist who had been keen on you once has just been awarded the Padma Bhushan."

"Masi, what a long obituary that illustrious author has got in today's papers—the one whom you had rejected."

Had Minnie Tthamma ever regretted her spinsterhood? Kushi faintly remembered some people asking, "Why couldn't you get married?"

They had got a spirited rejoinder. "It is *didn't*, not *couldn't*."

It had been a conscious decision, perhaps under the circumstances.

Minnie Tthamma (as well as her siblings) had been born into a Brahmo family. That is, their father had been a member of the Brahmo Samaj started in the 19th century by Raja Ram Mohan Roy.

She had lost her parents in her student days and had to shoulder the responsibilities of her many siblings. She got the whole brood educated and established in their respective slots, including Kushi's grandmother, the youngest of them. For that, she had to take up a post away from Calcutta, that of a headmistress in a school at Chittagong. She lived away from her siblings and yet, not just financed them but maintained close touch with them. The Partition of India had made her set up afresh in Rajpur. But she did it with fresh enthusiasm. Kushi had always found her full of energy and her house, of sun and air. "Always keep the doors and windows of mind open...," she said to Kushi. "Never shut them down."

Was that partly why it hurt to be kept out of the wider world Rahul was so much a part of?

She had taught Kushi how to write her capital letters, and to draw eggs. "You must put a little light blue into the eggs, and never leave it all white. You see, eggs reflect the sky. An *anda* is Brahmanda itself."

She had taught so much more. The soil of Rajpur was arid but Minnie Tthamma and the old gardener (with Jalpa around to help) had really worked on it. Kushi remembered the names; 'Love Lies Bleeding' that poured out its red-tipped stalk like a waterfall, and the 'Kiss Me Quick' that spread itself ingratiatingly on the ground. Minnie Tthamma had once caught her plucking off flowers thoughtlessly and taught her how to first see which ones were ready for the vase or the bowl and which ones needed more time on the stem.

In turn, she had taught Kuto never to tear off flowers and leaves from potted plants – anywhere.

Her father had his quarters some distance off, within the compounds of the Rajpur College. Ma did not have continuity in her stay here. Tthamma was ill so often! Becoming increasingly an invalid, needing her more and more!

Kushi's relationship with Rajpur was thus an on-and-off one. She was not a local, like Tapen or Lila, but she did have her associations here.

The continuous chirp of cricket was almost plugging Kushi's ears up. Then came the sudden whistle of the Upper India Express as it rushed by like an unseen genie shaking the foundations of the house.

For a minute she felt terrified–appalled. How had her grand-aunt borne it, night after night, year after year? For more than two decades? Hadn't she felt scared? Of thieves, house-breakers or, well, ghosts? Didn't she sometimes wake up in the middle of the night and feel insecure? Or regret that she had not built up a family of her own? A husband, even if he was a dotard or a drunkard? A son, even a retard, who lived under the same roof? Didn't she have moments of envy when neighbours talked of people under the same roof – even if they happened to be old husbands, unemployed sons, rude daughters-in-law or daughters thrown-out of their marital homes?

There was no way of knowing. For one fine day, Minnie Tthamma was struck by paralysis and had to be brought to Kolkata to her younger brother's place. She spent the next three years of her life wheel-chair-bound and dependent in an uncomprehending way. Her limbs had gone numb and her tongue stiff.

Kushi visited her at her grand-uncle's place where she knew she was receiving the best handling ever. But she saw that the bouquets from the Kolkata pavements brought no sparkle to her dull eyes. She had no earth here to grow things in – to plant and water and see them blossom like her students. Even her sky was scratched by electric wires and antennae, her air racked by crows and loudspeakers.

At Rajpur

Kushi sat holding her paralyzed hands but with anger against the Brahman or whatever was the power that had brought her to this state - with the soul being trapped within the body. Couldn't 'He' have let her die a quick death at Rajpur instead of this lingering one at Calcutta, done out of all the dignity and independence that she had stood for so far?

It was agony for Kushi to see in the clouded eyes a desperate desire for freedom and in her incoherent gurgle a cry to break away. *If I could, I would, this very instant, get on to the loop line train.*

Maybe she did get here, as soon as she was free from her body, thought Kushi, and is even now hovering about her garden, floating about the house, peering into the depths of the well, haunting Rajpur but in a happy way. Then came another thought. Perhaps that is why I got the idea of coming down here. It was she who messaged me!

With that, she closed her eyes and finally fell asleep.

✳ ✳ ✳

Birdsong, the roar of engines, and a whole new day! Kushi sat on the balcony, ruminating.

Ma often sent Kushi to see Minnie Tthamma's place while she did her cooking and cleaning in Baba's own quarters, and perhaps to find some time for themselves. But she called Tapen all the way over from his place, so near Minnie Tthamma's, to take Kushi there on his cycle. He was further to bring her back in the evening – and only then go all the way back home. Perhaps Ma did it because of her slight heart problem. Well, Tapen did not actually seem to mind the doubling of his efforts.

She remembered one chat they had had while cycling. They were both in their teens by then.

"Where are you going off to, after your Higher Secondary is over?" she had asked Tapen.

"What do you mean– where I am off to?"

"Like going to the Durgapur Regional Engineering College or the Shibpur Engineering College? Or, better still, the I.I.T.s?" "I'll stick to Rajpur, I think," Tapen had answered. "But what prospects does Rajpur have? And even otherwise, don't you want to see the world a bit?"

"I don't want to leave my parents alone, you know. My father is not keeping too well. My mother needs me at every step. Besides, what's wrong with Rajpur College? I'll do my B.Sc. there."

"Not one for travelling much, are you? Well, I am different. I can't think of being cooped up in one place for long. I want to see the world. I want to go places. Not just holidaying or shopping, but exploring old ruins or wild stretches."

There had been a sudden clap of thunder and within seconds, torrential rain. The landscape had gone obscure. Tapen's bicycle had wobbled and almost crashed. But he had clutched her and secured her to himself. She remembered that feeling – the smell of Lifebuoy soap that had not floated away in the last several years.

This evening Tapen took her to a roadside tea shop. Sitting on rickety benches, they had crisp fries and tea in little earthen pots. "Nothing like the *bhander cha*," said Kushi. "*Kulhad chai*, they call it in the north. Oh, I love it."

"Why did you ever stop coming to Rajpur?" Tapen asked with a smile.

"Oh, there were lots of things that happened...when I was in tenth grade and you perhaps in eleven. Minnie Tthamma had a paralytic stroke and was brought to Kolkata where it would be easier for everybody to take care of her. The house here was left for Jalpa's father to take care of."

"Ah, yes, I remember your mother writing to my parents if they could see to building an outhouse for his family."

"Meanwhile, I had the Higher Secondary coming up."

"Then?"

"With my grandparents getting sicker, Baba just had to shift closer to Kolkata."

"Rajpur faded away."

"Sort of...And then came college life, and marriage, you know."

"Ah, that part of the story I do know. You had come here once after your marriage."

Yes, of course. She had seen Tapen cycling by Minnie-Tthamma's house and called out to him. Tapen had stopped but had not really been too pleased to see her, she had thought for a second. But he was all politeness as Kushi, glowing with happiness, had introduced Rahul to him. "Call him Rahul, please," she had said again and again. But Tapen had refused to go on first-name terms with him. He had seemed to shrink a little away from the two of them.

"It has hardly changed, this place," she had remarked chattily. "This road is still *kachha*, you know."

"I do. I use it every day," Tapen had smiled.

Rahul had inquired about what Tapen did for his livelihood and how far away he stayed. Tapen had explained that he lived down the lane only a few houses behind. He had lost his father recently and now lived there with his mother. He had graduated from Rajpur College and was working with a private insurance company. Rahul had offered him a cigarette – a foreign brand. But Tapen had smiled it away. "It's only *bidi* with me."

He had not visited them again during the weekend that Kushi had stayed at Rajpur.

"How do you like Rajpur?" she had asked Rahul.

"I love it here," he had answered, "For, you are here." Indeed, he had not been keen to go around Rajpur much, refusing even to go up to see the trains. What is more, he had broken out in rashes after a bath in well-water, or so he felt.

She herself had not visited Rajpur since even when she had later come to Kolkata. Her parents had seen to the maintenance of the house but had hardly travelled down there, even after her father had inherited it. He said that it made him feel too nostalgic for the life he had had to give up. Payments to the caretakers, first

Jalpa's father and then Jalpa, were made mainly through money orders. Occasional repairs were through letters to Tapen's father and then to Tapen.

And, in any case, Kushi had become too wrapped up in her own family life by then.

"Like to go to the village tomorrow?" Tapen asked. "I am free. It's Sunday."

※ ※ ※

Early next morning, they started, Kushi riding behind Tapen in his cycle – 'double carrying' as they used to put it earlier.

The town of Rajpur gave way to paddy fields, irregular-shaped and separated by raised borders of earth called *aal*.

From the cycle manoeuvring the *aal*s, Kushi touched the paddy stalks.

"Peasants here still use cattle to plough the land," Tapen said. "No tractors on this sub-divided and fragmented land."

The local production of paddy, Kushi thought, was probably collected and stored in the tin sheds seen on the way from the railway station. They must ultimately be taken to the Food Corporation of India towering near Naraina in Delhi.

Tapen's small mobile rang out. He stretched out a foot and stopped the bicycle to answer it. Well, ninety *per cent* of rural India, Kushi knew, now had mobile services.

"Yes, Ma. I'll bring Kushi over to see you."

He handed her a lump of *gur* or jaggery from his *jhola*. "Made locally."

Kushi bit into it as Tapen resumed cycling.

At one point, they moved away from the paddy fields and reached a cowshed. The milkman was pulling at the swollen teats of a cow. Jets of milk were falling into an enamel bucket below, *Chyan Chun Chyan Chun...* The first sounds soon developed into *Gabur gubur gabur gubur* as the bucket began to fill up – like Kushi's heart with a certain joy.

"What do you do with all this milk?" Kushi asked.

The milkman explained that earlier he used to take it around directly to local people but now he takes most of it to the cooperative society developing in their district. He offered them two foaming pots of milk. Village courtesy alongside the White Revolution!

Tapen now cycled past the village pond, with a net cast into it and propped by poles. A signboard read, *The Fisheries Department of the Government*. Was a Blue Revolution also around the corner?

"Look, there's little Kopai," Tapen pointed to a stream flowing by with Taal or Palm trees on her banks. Had the *gur* that Tapen had given her come from the sap of these very trees?

It was getting hot. In the quiet of the countryside, Kushi could hear a hammering. Tapen explained that it was the local blacksmith. Though most of the villagers had turned away from metal utensils and instruments, he still had some business. It was the same story about the weaver and the potter in the village.

Kushi felt that the old self-sufficiency of the Indian village was not entirely gone. She recalled Government efforts in reviving the village through providing outlets such as in the Craft Museum, the Dilli Haats and the Surajkund Craft Mela. A new interest in these aspects began to grow in her. There was so much more to life than one's own narrow grooves.

Before Kushi's eyes, a *bhand* or pot was fast taking shape on the potter's wheel. Kushi brought out her smartphone and took a video clip. "For my friend Veena," she told Tapen. "She's a social worker. Very much 'into' things ethnic. Always goes for *kulhad chai*s."

The village was not too far from the coal fields that overlapped West Bengal and Jharkhand.

"In spite of accidents that occur, villagers do go over to the mining areas in search of work," said Tapen. "There are 'light industries' here like rice mills, sugar mills and saw mills. As for 'heavy industries', villagers have gone to Durgapur Steel Plant— and Burnpur too. Some such heavy industrial units are coming up here as well." He pointed at some factory building a little way off – almost right out of the paddy fields.

"What about air and noise pollution and industrial disasters?" said Kushi. "Veena is so critical of the way industrialization is taking place in our country."

"It *is* a twisted tale," admitted Tapen.

He stopped before a cluster of huts, with a couple of bigger buildings, newly constructed. Tapen rattled the latch of a hut with a *shouchalaya* or toilet at the back – almost into the fields.

The household members cast curious looks at Kushi but obviously knew Tapen. They welcomed them in with a homemade *nimbu-pani*, and offered them lunch.

A slim, dark girl served them on the floor as per the village custom. Polished brass *thali*s and wavy-edged brass *katoras* piled up with coarse rice, thick pulses and mixed vegetables. The girl also brought sliced lemons and homemade pickles. Her mother sat nearby and fanned them with a palm-leaf fan edged with a *sari* border. There was a table fan, Kushi noticed, and a light bulb as well. The village was electrified but there must be a power failure now.

"Good that it is a holiday for her and she did not have to go to that school of hers," said the mother.

Kushi looked up, surprised.

Tapen volunteered the information, "Neera is a schoolteacher. She teaches at the *Prathamik Vidyalaya* here."

"That's all due to you, Dada," said Neera. "You coached me for my B. Ed and you talked to the Secretary of the Governing Body." "*Arrey*, I knew him and I just mentioned you to him, that's all," Tapen said gruffly. "No, no," he stopped Neera from piling more rice onto his *thali*.

Earlier, there had only been a *pathshala* in the village. But now there was a primary school with government assurances of a bigger school under the Board of Secondary Education, West Bengal.

A small child came out from somewhere in the house – just about Kuto's age – Kushi thought. But he was rubbing his eyes and squinting.

Tapen took a small bottle of eye-drops out of his pocket and handed them to Neera.

"It's in short supply and that is why the Primary Health Centre did not have it. Requisition it, and ask Billu not to go playing near that factory."

He explained that a new factory building was coming up close by and its building material raised dust that was harmful to the eyes. Several villagers who lived nearby had developed itching eyes and even blurred vision. Tapen had made the villagers complain and get a stay order from the local court. But children often played hide-and-seek among its half-built walls. This child, a younger brother of Neera's, had sensitive eyes and was among the villagers affected.

Kushi washed her hands in the water that Neera poured out for her from a brass pot. "Do you like your job?"

She nodded happily.

"I'll show you the school from outside since it is Sunday today."

After using the newly-constructed *shouchalaya* or toilet at the back of the house, Kushi took leave of the household.

"Neera, go along with them," said Neera's parents, as they left.

✱ ✱ ✱

Neera walked with the two of them, Tapen walking his cycle. Midway they came upon a tall youth on a bike. His features were half-hidden under his unruly hair and unkempt beard. He was in *kurta-pajama*, *jhola* and *hawai chappa*ls. He dismounted and said, "*Namaste.*"

"Ah, Alex! Back from the church? Come, meet a Didi from India's capital."

The three of them walked together for a while. Then, with a slight bow, Alex mounted his bike and took off in a different direction.

After a few more steps Neera showed Kushi the school building. Through its windows, Kushi saw the simple classrooms with rough-hewn benches and tables, and small square blackboards. Many girls from the village, Neera said, have started to come here, even if it was only for the Mid-Day Meal Scheme. Kushi had a sudden desire to get in and begin teaching here, filling the blackboard with lines of chalk, and then wiping them off and writing afresh. Like she used to do once with water on the rough floors of the house in Kolkata. It would be fun! She had not felt any sense of fun for long.

Next to the school was the Primary Health Centre of the village.

"Children come here for DPT shots and oral Polio vaccines, and for anti-venom serum," Neera paused and glanced at Tapen.

"Remember Alex's case, Dada?"

Alex was a volunteer of the church missionaries in the district. Last monsoon, he had been wading through the watery paddy fields when he had been bitten by a snake. In spite of the rain, the villagers had taken him to the Primary Health Centre in an open cart. But there they found that the Centre was out of anti-venom serum. They were at a loss for what to do. Tapen, who was cycling by in the rain, had come upon Alex, lying on an open cart with the rain pouring upon him. He had driven ahead of the cart and guided the villagers to the district hospital or '*bado haaspatal*' as it was called.

That is how Tapen had come to be so well-regarded in the village.

He was at present actively campaigning for the *Swachh Bharat Abhiyan* (SBA) or *Swachh Bharat Mission* (SBM), and persuading villagers to change their old, unhygienic habits.

Bringing all this about, in addition to doing his own job, looking after his old mother, and helping neighbours with maintenance and other odd jobs! Kushi felt Tapen was quite a hero – though completely unsung.

Tapen got onto the bicycle and she behind him. Neera went home after many requests to Kushi to come again.

Kushi could feel the sun on her back mellowing. She saw villagers getting back from Rajpur and other work places. Evening came with conch shells and temple bells sounding, cows mooing as they were tied up in their sheds, and lights twinkling, though few and far, between the darkening fields.

Cycling became easier as they reached the smooth road to the town, and soon they were at Minnie Tthamma's place. "Tomorrow you must come and see Ma, and have lunch there," said Tapen as he rode away.

Once in, she switched her phone on. Data usage, of course, no question of Wi-Fi here.

What a lot of WhatsApp photos there were from Rahul! Even videos. They seemed so unreal. She glossed over them and passed on to the message from Veena, rather, from Kuto.

"Mummy, how are you? I am fine. Veena Aunty is nice. But when are you going to be back?"

Ah, Kuto…

The crickets were creating a thick, impenetrable barrier against the world she had left behind. The deafening sound of silence shut out everything else…

By the time Jhumri called her to the dining table for two, the electricity failed. Jhumri brought a lantern.

Many must have been the nights Minnie Tthamma had taken her solitary dinner on this table, with the lantern casting strange shadows on the walls.

✳ ✳ ✳

The next day, she charged her phone, bathed and walked about the garden. Around eleven, Tapen came to pick her up. She thought of handing some cash to Tapen for the repairs to be done on the house. But she had come on the spur of the moment and did not have enough cash with her. Nor did she have an account here, though there was a well-known bank with its branch here. Did it have an ATM? She had not noticed. But Tapen proudly

At Rajpur

said yes and took Kushi to the bank where she used her debit card with a sort of wonder. Services here have been picking up indeed.

As she stepped out of the ATM, she saw an old village woman bump hard into a scooter carelessly parked outside. Tapen helped her up and put her on a cycle-rickshaw. "Isn't it that old Motimasi whose mango grove you boys once used to raid?"

"Yes. But she has smartened up. She no longer keeps her money hidden in holes in her floor but uses the bank."

Kushi handed over some cash to Tapen and explained its purpose. Tapen nodded and then cycled with her to his home.

A simple single-storied house, but well cared-for and in good condition.

Tapen's mother was in a borderless white sari for widows. Her hair was grey and her gait was stiff. Kushi bent to touch her feet but she drew Kushi up and wanted to know every detail of the past decade from her. Kushi showed her almost the entire gallery on her smartphone.

"What a good-looking husband! What a beautiful child!" she exclaimed between her condolences about Kushi's parents. "Can't cook as well as I used to," she said, serving her lunch. "And that boy of mine does not even notice what I put before him. Not much fun cooking in such a situation."

Kushi admired all her vegetable dishes, and the recipes came rushing out, also that of the *mishti-doi*. Tapen ate with her but got up and left for some work he had to finish before he took Kushi back. Tapen's mother suggested that she had a nap on her bed. Kushi was so replete that she did feel a bit drowsy, and agreed.

The two of them lay down on a simple four-poster. Not the Burma teak affair of Minnie Tthamma, but big and broad. It was comfortable and with Tapen's mother lying down beside her, chewing *paan* and talking about recipes, she felt herself going into a snooze.

Then she heard Tapen's mother hiss at her ear. "Now tell me, Kushi, why exactly you are here."

Shaken out of her drowsiness, she could only say, "Just for a change, *Mashima*."

"Not had a tiff with your husband, have you?"

"No, Mashima," Kushi said quite truthfully. It was worse, she knew. Not being able even to have one.

"Well, it must be something – for a young mother to leave her son with a friend and come down to this dump?"

There was no softness in her voice.

Kushi tried to explain. "Mashima, I just felt cooped up. I just wanted a change."

"Cooped up, there? Came for a change, here?"

Her voice was acidic.

"I will be going back in a couple of days…"

"That's why, Kushi, I am scared. I have been noticing my son ever since you came. His eyes have got back the shine I never saw in them since you left. But you will leave again. What would happen to him then?"

"Mashima, I never…"

"I know. You never. But that's why, you should leave as early as you can. Why raise false hopes? Why tempt?"

No afternoon nap was possible after this. Kushi mumbled something but Tapen's mother put her hand up in a gesture of denial.

"What did you think of Neera?" she said.

"Neera?"

"Yes, you met her yesterday – Tapen told me."

"Oh, that Neera!"

"Yes, I wouldn't mind having her as a *bou*."

Kushi shook herself into making a cheerful reply, "Yes, Mashima. You do need a daughter-in-law and she seems just right."

"So, don't come in between them. Even before they are together."

Thankfully, it was past afternoon and she heard Tapen come back.

With a complete change of manner, Tape's mother handed her a packet.

"A gift for you. Guess from whom? Your Minnie Tthamma!"

They were some old letters that she had kept with Tapen's mother. She had not wanted them to fall into the hands of her relatives once she had passed away. But she had not wanted to destroy them either. "Just keep them somewhere …for Kushi when she grows up. Maybe she will find them interesting, maybe not. But no others, I say."

Did she then have a premonition of her paralysis?

For soon after, Minnie Tthamma had been taken to Calcutta where she eventually passed away.

"You never visited me after your wedding, even when you came here. I know you did – Tapen had told me. But now I must hand it over. Who knows when my own time will be up?"

Kushi touched her feet as she left.

"Next time, don't come alone," Mashima lightly touched her chin and brought the fingers to her lips in an old-world gesture.

❋ ❋ ❋

"If you are not in a hurry, we can go and watch the trains again," said Tapen as they reached Minnie Tthamma's house.

They sat waiting for the next train to come, either way. Kushi clutched the packet in her hand. Tapen lit a *bidi*.

"Yesterday's trip to the village –how did you like it?" Tapen began.

"I wish I didn't have come to come back," said Kushi with a catch in her voice. "Remember *Kapalakundala* by Bankim Chandra Chattopadhyaya? The heroine - Kapalakundala– brought up on a deserted island – says after getting a taste of married life that - happiness for her would mean wandering once again along the beaches by herself. That's the kind of happiness I felt yesterday."

"That's just a novel, you know."

"No. It is reality. Kapalakundala says that she has come to realize that marriage for a woman is servitude, and had she known that earlier, she would not have gotten married at all. That's exactly how I feel."

"That's a strong statement. What's wrong, Kush?"

Kush? Tapen had never used endearments before. Kushi tried to check her rising tears and say, in a matter-of-fact tone, "I have made a mess of my life and you are as much to blame."

"How so? How can I be responsible for the mess — even if *you* have made one out of your life?"

He tried to keep his tone light but Kushi turned halfway towards him and put her arms around him, *bidi* and all.

"Why did you ever let me go? Why did you allow me to move away from here?"

She felt him stiffen and whisper, "Just what do you mean by that?"

"You could have kept me here, you know, had you once told me that you loved me. I wouldn't have gone away then."

"Wait a minute. What did you say about my loving you?"

"Look. Tapen, don't deny it. Even my mother used to joke that you were my boyfriend and that is why you were remaining a bachelor. And your mother today—" she stopped abruptly.

Tapen broke away from her and gave a hoot of laughter.

"I sort of thought she would. But you, Kushi, you know better than to listen to mothers and aunts match-making and imagining things, don't you?"

The earth began to vibrate with an approaching train.

"Is it entirely that, Tapen?"

"Well, supposing it isn't? What then?"

"Then you have been very silly and mucked up my life as well as yours. Had you just told me once, I would have done something about it."

"Like what?"

"I would have insisted that you join some engineering college – if not the IITs then the regional engineering college, say, at Durgapur. Get out of here and move ahead in life. So that one day we could…"

"…reach exactly where you are now at – with your Rahul."

In the dark, a train was approaching from the Rajpur side. Its light was getting bigger and bigger, its whistling louder and louder.

"Would you have me staying here with you, oiling my hair, bathing in well water, cooking alongside your mother, going to the local *haat* and sometimes to the local cinema hall? I would have done it all. If you had only asked me…"

"Enough."

Bur Kushi went on. "Our child could have toddled along the red earth and across paddy fields."

"You are saying that now. Would you have said it then?"

"But why didn't *you* say it then? You had plenty of opportunities – in the evenings we cycled or sat watching the trains."

Vibrations again. Another train was coming – this time from the other side. Kushi could see its lights through a blur of tears.

"You have deprived me. All these years," Kushi said.

"Deprived? You? Of what?"

"Of you, you fool!"

The train – a goods wagon – rattled its way beneath. Then there was a silence. But Tapen spoke soon again.

"You have never exactly been deprived of that, you know. You have had it all along. It is not my fault that you have never known or needed it – before now."

"Well, I need it now."

"You do?"

"That's what I have come here for. I have been trying to tell you that ever since I came."

He pulled her close now, with the accumulated force of years. Her lips met his lined forehead and then bit into his tired mouth.

"You would never speak," she said once she was through that one.

"Why did I have to speak to be heard?"

"Your first kiss, is it? I see you do not know how."

"It is indeed my first kiss but it could be better on a second attempt."

When she freed herself, she was breathless. But could not help asking, "Neera?"

"Neera?"

"Isn't there something between you – something growing?"

"I will have to see to it that she marries Alex," he laughed, "who loves her but who belongs to another faith."

"But…Mashima…she has other ideas."

"She may, but that does not mean they are going to work out."

"But she is getting on... and needs a daughter-in-law."

"Well, she must wait till I need a wife."

"Don't you, Tapen?"

"Not as yet, Kushi."

"But don't you feel lonely? Don't you want someone by your side?"

"I have memories. They keep me company."

"But you can't get anywhere with memories! You can't go ahead holding on to a spectre's hand!"

"I don't think I want to go anywhere, to get on."

"Not even with me?

"Especially not with you."

"But why?"

"Because, as you said, one can't go forward holding a spectre's hand."

"I am not a spectre—"

"You are. Looking back at its old past–trying to re-enter its dead body."

He paused and added, "But I have never left my body. I am where I have always been. Even if I held your hand, you would flit by – like the dream girl you have always been to me."

Another train came by… cutting through the darkness that had descended.

They both knew the time it passed here - had always done. It was around ten in the night.

They got up to go, Kushi carefully holding her packet.

Jalpa had the light on at the verandah. Like a beacon in the sea.

At the gate, Tapen said, "Evening tomorrow, after office."

Kushi nodded in the dark and crunched away into the house.

The dinner was piping hot chicken curry but she was rather full. She switched on her smart phone and found videos of Kuto and Rahul. Sent through WhatsApp, they seemed to be from another world, making their way through the dense wall of crickets' chirp. She opened the packet and turned to the letters.

Senhora Das

Das had been her grandmother's maiden name. So naturally that is how Minnie Tthamma would be addressed in Portuguese, was it?

Senhora Das

I was appalled to hear of the impending political event. The Partition of India seems to be nothing short of a disaster. I am all the more troubled because these are turbulent times. Are you sure you have taken the right decision in moving away from Chittagong? From your own life's work? The school will not be the same without you as its headmistress.

Of course, I will continue to stay in the country where I had found myself in, by favour of my ancestors who had arrived here around 1512.

I have been born and brought up here. I am a Firangi of Patharghatta. I have always attended church at the Cathedral of Our Lady of the Holy Rosary at Bandel Road, been taken into its fold early in my youth. Do write again and tell me about your life there - wherever you have retired to. Let me end with something that I hope Our Lady of the Holy Rosary will forgive me for saying. Tenho saudades tuas. Padre Costa, SJ

Kushi turned to another of the letters.

Senhora Das, but permit me to say, Minha Querida.

Thank you for writing 'Amaro apnar katha khub mone hoi', which is what is the closest you can get to Tenho saudades tuas. It is strange that when we reveal our mutual feelings, we have to use a language that one knows and the other does not. Well, that is why there are dictionaries, I guess.

It is wonderful that your relatives are getting you a plot of land in a small town that is more like the countryside. Good that they will also build a small house on the plot, and settle you down there.

One part of me has to write this. But there is another part which says: why did you have to go so far away from here.

From your school? No, that's not the whole truth. From me.

I remember the first time I saw you. You had come with a small batch of your students to show them the Portuguese influences that still remained in Chittagong—in the cathedral, for example.

There are families from Bengal here. I know what a Bengali lady looks like and how she moves about. You were not quite that. I recognized that you were a specimen of the modern young Indian woman. Educated, fluent in English, and spirited enough to take up a job far away from home.

And so beautiful.

In my forty years, I had never found a woman beautiful.

There were certain stirrings in me that I had never known myself to have.

I offered to show you and your students around the cathedral. Then to a few other buildings that I knew were there, but perhaps not in good condition – or safe enough for visitors. We started chatting.

That is how I came to know you. You were more than smart and beautiful. You were brave and dedicated to a cause. You also had a burden on your slim shoulders. You had lost your parents early and had to finance the education and upkeep of your young siblings – earning more here than you could have done in Bengal. You belonged to a reformist faith that was your own strength.

More than ten years my junior, you made me admire you.

I have been admiring you for the two whole decades that have passed after that. You know it now. Or perhaps you have always known it?

Padre Costa, SJ

Kushi had been brought up to have qualms about reading the letters of others. But these were letters that her grand-aunt had wanted her to read, to share across time, through the wall of crickets chirping away in the darkness outside.

How had her grand-aunt spent night after night here? Was it with the help of these letters? She wondered as she fell asleep.

※ ※ ※

Her sleep was broken by slivers of sunlight through the windows and loud calls from Jhumri.

"Didi, there's someone to see you."

It took Kushi only a few minutes to brush her teeth, and change, and come out to the balcony. It was later than the usual time she got up. The light outside was brilliant.

A youthful figure in *kurta-pajama* stood there, with features half-hidden under unruly hair and beard. A side-bag on his shoulders, and rubber sandals on his feet. Kushi knew who he was even before he had said *Namaste*, bringing his hands together.

Jalpa too was there. "Tapen Dada has sent him. *E* Jhumri, get the tea!"

"*Arre*, there's no time for tea," Alex said.

Tapen had sent him to pick Kushi up and take her to the fields she had visited earlier. There was an urgent situation, and Tapen was right there. But he was calling for Kushi.

"Sure, but how can I – what can I—"

"Didi, just come. There's my bike."

Alex smiled persuasively, showing up two canine teeth and two light brown eyes in a bearded face with a hawk-like nose.

Kushi did as she was told. The bike hurtled through Rajpur towards the fields that lay beyond. The breeze –still cool – carried back snatches of what Alex was saying. "Waste stuff from that new factory... flooded the fields...you are to send a report to Delhi."

"I... But..."

The bike sped on. Now it was travelling on the earthen mounds or dividers between the fields... balancing itself precariously. Kushi kept quiet, just taking in the green of the landscape she was passing through.

The bike came to an abrupt halt. "Look!" Alex pointed down at the fields.

Kushi gasped. The crops stood inch-deep in thick, black, shiny stuff that had a strong chemical odour. And, it was rising, creeping up!

A few villagers stood on the *aals*, slapping their foreheads. Tapen too was there, and with her arms around a wailing village woman, wasn't that Neera?

"What is it? Where's it coming from?" a bewildered Kushi asked.

Neera came forward. "Oh, good, Didi, you have come."

She articulated – what Kushi had by now figured out. This was an industrial waste – toxic effulgence –released out of the factory being set up some way off from the fields. It had pipes releasing its waste material and some of them must have been running along the sides of the fields. Sometime in the night, one or more of those pipes must have burst at the seams and the waste they were carrying had entered the field, seeping in through the soil or spilling out through some hole in the ground.

"Kushi, don't just stand there looking dazed," said Tapen. "Get your smartphone out and take pics – or even videos. None of us here have smartphones. Quick! Snap it up while it is still flowing in," he paused and went on more quietly.

"I have called a journalist friend who works with a local daily. I am also trying to get to the big, Kolkata-based dailies. But this is not a local matter. The factory has been set up by a big corporation. I want you to get to the *Indian Express*, the *Times of India*, the *Hindustan Times, India Today* or the *Down To Earth* … and I want to get to them fast. You have a smartphone! I noticed it that day when you had come. Can't you also send an on-the-spot report? Of course, you can."

"Wait a bit," began Kushi in an uncertain voice.

But Alex spoke out, "Didi, do we have the time to wait?"

Kushi saw the point. If an immediate report was not made, the matter would get dated and delayed and perhaps lost. "Write something out," she told Tapen, while she quickly took some clips of the fields inundated with industrial waste, of the pipes running too close to them, of the spot where they had burst, and of the factory raising its head and encroaching upon agricultural land.

Tapen soon handed her over a bit of notepaper where he had written out the report. In Bengali. Neera and Alex put in a few more details. Kushi translated and typed it out on her phone and sent it by email as well as WhatsApp to good old Veena.

"Thank God for data usage," she thought. There might be a cybercafé or two in Rajpur town, but it would take so long to go back, locate them, and perhaps find that the Internet was down!

More villagers had come up through the fields. They were talking about the loss that the industrial waste, creeping up the paddy stalks, would make. Three men came from the Rajpur side as well. All of them, *jhola*-types. Local "party" people, it seemed, with three different political affiliations. Tapen talked to one, ignoring the others. One of them had a camera and took photographs as well as notes. A reporter from the local newspaper?

Her smartphone rang. Veena sounded excited about the email that had reached her. She asked for a few more details and Kushi gave the phone over to Tapen. He gave it to Alex who was the one to speak to Veena. His English sounded strangely impressive amidst the paddy stalks. The people around cast admiring glances.

Once Alex had given the phone back, she moved away to the road. Neera walked along with her. Alex too came along. Kushi took a good look at them together. The way Alex looked at Neera and Neera at him…Well, Tapen's mother may have to wait awhile to have a daughter-in-law.

She waved at Tapen from afar and mounted the bike again. Alex sped away once again with her. She could not help asking him about his English, and he said: "I was brought up by the Fathers at St Xavier's, Rajpur. I am an orphan."

"But how is it that you landed up here?"

"I wanted to become a priest but the Fathers wanted me to work with people. They sent me to this area."

"And you have stayed on, in spite of the snakebite you nearly died from?"

"All the more. For, it showed me that it is in this area that I am needed."

Hmm. Veena was a social worker, with a degree from the Delhi School of Social Work. Here was another but without degrees.

"Well, you look every bit a villager," Kushi blurted out and felt sorry the next moment.

"That's the best way to work among them, to be one of them," Alex called back with a laugh.

He dropped Kushi and rushed off, refusing the tea Kushi offered.

But on her verandah, there was someone else sipping tea.

***

"I have been waiting all this while," said Lila, the childhood friend who had sent her some pickles almost as soon as she had arrived. She hugged Kushi and drew back.

"*Arre*, your *sari* border is wet – your feet are covered in slime. What's all this?"

Kushi quickly explained and Lila laughed.

"Aha – that is where you had gone, early in the morning. I have been observing you, Kushi, from my house. Going out with our Tapen every day, with never a moment to spare for your other friends!"

Lila had a laughing way with her, but Kushi did feel a bit self-conscious. Lila had been married off young. But she had not been accepted by her in-laws and had stayed on at her parental place. However, she still had a big *bindi* on and rather loud colours on her sari.

"I found time today and came over before you made off from here again! Decided to wait it out for you. *Ei* Jhumri, get us some more tea."

She exclaimed over all the pics of Rahul and Kuto that were there on the smartphone and squeezed as much information as she could about Kushi's life.

"How I envy you, Kushi!" she said at the end of it.

"The grass is always greener on the other side of the fence!" Kushi made a rejoinder.

"What if there is no grass on this side of the field?" Lila countered.

Her husband, she mentioned of her own accord, had remarried and even had a kid. Lila made a face... to suggest that she did not really care. Kushi wondered if it was indeed so but her thoughts soon returned to the fields inundated by sludge. Perhaps Lila sensed her lack of interest. For, she got up after a while, and left, asking Kushi to drop in at her place, that is, her parental place, close by, whenever she was free.

Kushi had a thorough bath and washed away the sludge from her petticoat and *sari* border. She gave it to Jhumri for a further wash at the well-side, and had an early lunch – Jhumri's simple preparations.

Then she settled down with the letters once again, on the sun-washed verandah.

Senhora, my very own Senhora,

Will you ever forgive me for the one sin I committed? On just that one evening in the Portuguese ruins near Patharghatta? My sin, not yours, though you did not resist, scream or succumb. You responded.

I felt every nerve of yours tingle with every touch of mine. I had not planned it, you had not either. But it had happened nevertheless. We did not know how, but it had. We never repeated it, nor did we refer to it till about four or five months later when I saw you bring your students again to show them around the cathedral. I was shocked to see your rounded contours. I was a priest but I was not blind. It was I who sent you a message to come and see me in the old ruins where we had both lost our heads.

"Don't worry," you told me. "I will give the baby away to my sister in Kolkata who is also expecting a baby around the same time. She will give it out that she has had twins. I have already applied for leave from the school."

"Let me leave the church," I said wildly. "I am ready to throw everything away for you," I cried.

"No," you said. "We both have our callings."

I wept but you had made up your mind. You did take some leave and go back to Kolkata for a while. Then I saw you come back, slim and shapely as before. You continued to visit the cathedral with your students and even talk to me. But you never met me alone again, never answered my appeals to come just once to the Pattharghatta ruins. Until, of course, the last time when you said you were retiring from the school and going back to what would be India, after the Transfer of Power.

Your hair was beginning to silver and both my eyes had cataracts. "What was 'it' and where is it now?" I asked – at last.

"A son. Of course, to him I am Minnie-masi. An aunt." I felt tears rising in my eyes and said, "He doesn't know?"

"Nobody knows but my sister. She will die with the secret."

That was not the last time we met, but it was the last time we met in private. You had come once more before you actually retired from service, and left Chittagong. You wrote once you reached Kolkata and gave me this address that I have been writing to ever since then. You were so formal, even cold, but then, why else did you write if you did not want me to write back?"

Kushi sat staring into the distance, her brows furrowed. Twin sons, twins! Why, that meant her own father and uncle. The sister – that was her own grandmother – Tthamma–who had indeed passed away with her secret.

No, it just can't be true.

Why, Minnie Tthamma had been the one to come up to Kolkata when the news about Molu Kaka had come. It was she who had calmed her own Tthamma down from a state of near hysteria. Molu Kaka's loss had not been of special concern to her…Or had it? Was it then that her first stroke had occurred– a mild one that she told relatives not to fuss about– followed a few years later by the second more severe one that brought her to their mercy?

✳ ✳ ✳

Kushi was still reeling from the shock of seeing her great-aunt in a completely different role, when, the next day, Jhumri asked her to come with her to a festive dance in the evening.

It was in honour of their deity Luguburu. Her people were getting together in a clearing by the rail-line, further up where the embankment came down to ground level. Kushi saw that, in spite of the missionary influence here, tribal gods had not been forgotten altogether. The spirit of Luguburu still hung around.

Kushi agreed.

Tapen would be dealing with those who must by now have gathered around the area contaminated with toxic effulgence, and had messaged that he would not be able to look her up today.

Jalpa and Jhumri finished off their work early and Kushi walked with them to the clearing where the dance was to take place. A number of people were already there, with their dark bodies, flattish noses, curly hair and bright smiles. The men had worn short, white *dhoti*s and tied colourful scarves around their waists and heads. The women had bead necklaces and flowers in their well-oiled hair. As Jalpa and Jhumri explained about Kushi, they giggled and got out a *chatai* or palm-leaf mat for Kushi to sit on.

As it grew dark, drums and flutes began to be heard. Men and women formed rows and began to dance. They held each other by the waist, going backwards and forwards. At the same time, they formed a slowly moving circle. It was a group dance with no one ahead of another, no one alone.

Do tribal societies here or anywhere in the world have solo dancing, like say, Kathak, developing ultimately into performances done for the stage? For entertainment or appreciation of others rather than the joy of it- a collective joy? Kushi wondered.

The line of dancers – with Jhumri among them - drew near Kushi. Jhumri stretched out a hand and pulled Kushi up. Kushi found herself dancing, with Jhumri on one side and an unknown girl on the other. They passed their hands through the loop her arms had automatically formed by touching the waist. She fell into their steps. In a little jumping step, she also moved sideways as well as forwards, with the rest keeping up with their monotone of "*Luguburu Ghantabari re...*"

Her heart began to thump a little – the reason why she had never been sent to dancing classes. But she felt like dancing forever.

There was some heavy scent in the air – was it Mahua wine or the blossoms themselves? There was no applauding audience. But the moon, coming up among the trees, was audience enough!

The chicken roast on open fire made for an ethnic barbecue.

It was midnight by the time they got back, swaying slightly on their feet. All through the neighbourhood, the lights had been switched off and households had sunk into slumber. Only a few street lights burnt in their lampshades of buzzing insects.

But as they drew closer, they saw that someone had got in through the gate, and switched the balcony light on. Kushi clenched her fists and blinked. The few sips of *mahua* must have got to her head. She must be hallucinating…But it *was* Rahul. In flesh.

Rahul was back.

When had he arrived and how had he got in?

He had arrived by the same train that Kushi had arrived by, taken a cycle-rickshaw and, after a few wrong turns, located the house. Finding the gate locked, and shouts un-answered, he had climbed over the gate. Then finding the house itself locked, he had settled down on the balcony, which had its light switch outside. His small suitcase on wheels stood there, still with its travel tags.

"Kuto?" Kushi could hardly hear her own voice.

Had anything happened to Kuto that Rahul had come down in person from wherever he was?

Rahul was quick to understand. "Oh, he's alright. Met him at Veena's and gave him his presents. Dumped the rest of the luggage there itself – and went to the railway station and jumped into this train – that I saw I could still catch."

Kushi, bent in the act of unlocking the door, asked in a muffled voice, "Why didn't you go home?"

"You know I don't like going home with you not there."

Kushi straightened up. Yes, this was one of Rahul's fads. He wanted Kushi to be there to open the door and let him in. He said he could not stand an empty house. Kushi had often felt the irony of this statement.

She threw open the door, switched on the light and let him in. Instantly, as was his habit, he knelt down before her on the floor. Automatically she kissed the top of his hair – smelling nice in spite of the train journey.

"You must be famished. Let me ask Jhumri to knock something up for you," she said.

"Sure – but tell me now, why are you here? Why had you come down here, and okay, even if you had done so for a bit of change, why hadn't you got back in time? Or at least messaged me? You knew I would be back last night."

Kushi could not tell him the truth – that it had slipped her mind. She was appalled herself. How could it have happened!

Jhumri had not waited for Kushi to tell her about getting some dinner for Rahul. Her bangles sounded on the door, and she brought in a platter of hot *chapati* and *achar* - something for the guest to bite into. Fortunate.

"How did your trip go?" Kushi asked as she did every time he came back from one.

"Great," said Rahul, in between the *chappati*s and *achar*. "Didn't you see the pics and the videos? Sent them all through. From every place I covered around Bombay."

It was true. But Kushi has just given them cursory glances. Why?

Rahul was tired, after all. He fell into the bed, and went to sleep with his shoes on.

Kushi pulled them out. The very same familiar ones she had helped to get polished.

She fitted herself into the bed – a single bed but of old-time proportions.

Tapen came quite early the next morning. Jalpa had run to his place as soon as it was light, and he came to inquire if anything was the matter and whether any help was needed. Like getting quick rail reservations back for the two of them together. He knew a local travel agent who could help.

He was courtesy itself but Kushi could see the sag of the shoulders, the droop of the lips. They had not been there when he had stood before the contaminated fields among bewildered villagers, thinking of how to tackle the situation. She knew Rahul had brought them to him – by his unexpected arrival.

Perhaps because Tapen's voice had carried, Rahul got up. Kushi saw him come out to the balcony where Tapen and she were talking.

Tapen did a *Namaste* while Rahul – yawning – stretched out a hand. He obviously remembered that they had met when Kushi and Rahul had come down here after her wedding. Hadn't he teasingly referred to him just the other day as 'the Rajpur one'?

They exchanged civilities and inquiries. Rahul jumped at the offer of Tapen helping with the tickets.

"As early as possible – first class, of course – and anything else that's needed," said Rahul, bringing out a handful of notes. "I hope there is an ATM here. I don't have too many rupees on me. Had not thought it would be necessary when I landed at Delhi airport."

Tapen smiled and asked Rahul to let the money be for the present. "Kushi has placed a lot with me for repairs. I have enough for the tickets."

He made a move to go but Kushi spoke out. "Wait a bit. I am not going back—"

Tapen stopped stock-still. Rahul's yawn turned into a gasp.

"—just now," she completed her sentence. "I have something to settle here and someone to talk to before I go."

"Oh, okay!" Rahul laughed. "For a moment I thought you meant you were not coming back at all."

Tapen's body too had relaxed. He smiled, and asked, "Who is this someone you must talk to before you go?"

"And what is this matter that you must settle?" asked Rahul, yawning again.

Her smartphone rang with a WhatsApp message. Veena had just sent the screenshots of the reports of the Rajpur disaster that had appeared in two of the national dailies to which she had sent it. As she handed the phone to Tapen, and he looked into it, she saw his face light up.

Jhumri brought tea and Rahul, all politeness, insisted on Tapen taking at least a sip before leaving.

"Can you ask Alex to see me sometime today?" Kushi called out after him.

Puri-tarkari appeared on the small dining table inside, which had two people sitting at it again.

Rahul polished it all off and said, "And now for the news. Prime Time news. Kushi, my Khushi, we are going to Bangkok!"

Rahul had wangled a contract at a prestigious institute there – a dream job by all standards, though time-bound.

"I couldn't wait to tell you!"

So, it was not just that he could not bear to enter a home without Kushi. It was this grand piece of news that he could not keep to himself.

Kushi found herself saying, "Oh great, but when do you have to go?"

"Idiot! It's not just me – you, and Kuto as well. The family! It's a posting, not a tour. The contract is with the company – lending me, as it were, for two years."

It sunk in gradually. Vistas of air travel, overseas journeys to unknown parts of the world unfolded before her…so many rushing images that there was no room for expression on her face. Details followed. The long and short of it was that the offer had to be taken up immediately, say, within the month.

Kushi succumbed to the lure of distant lands and of Rahul's closeness. Wasn't this her dream always? How lucky she was!

All day they discussed how to make it work. There were so many details to attend to.

But one part of Kushi's brain was busy elsewhere.

Rahul fell asleep again, even though it was early evening. He had given his news, told his story, and now was utterly relaxed.

Not Kushi.

✼ ✼ ✼

As soon as Alex came crunching up the gravel in the evening, she rushed to the balcony.

"You called for me? To know what's happening there at ground level?"

He began on an animated report.

Kushi gazed at him. Yes, light eyes, hawk-like features, and canine teeth that made the smile extra attractive.

Alex was holding forth on the injustice big industrial houses did to small farmers. Kushi broke in.

"Alex, have you read *Alice in Wonderland*?"

"Yes, of course," Alex stared.

"Did you read it at your school library? Did the Fathers have it there?"

"No, I had my own copy. It was the only thing I had of my own when the Fathers had taken me in. I refused to part with it," he grinned. "I still have the book if you want a sudden look."

"Your parent's gift to you?"

"Actually, no. It was a sister's gift – which I clung to even when my own parents dumped me."

"So, you had a sister of your own?"

"No, a cousin. Her name's there in the book. She got it as a prize from her school. That's what made the book so special."

Kushi gripped the edge of the balcony and asked, "Hadn't you ever tried to find her out? You had the name."

"The Fathers said that it was my parents' insistence that I do not try to trace any of my family. They had cut themselves off from it, and I was to do the same. That's how they wanted it."

Kushi remembered her father looking at the old albums and tried to check her rising tears.

"It was their last and only wish as the Fathers told me, and I have always respected it. But why do you—"

"Yes, yes, I know. I shouldn't be asking all this and making it worse for you. But tell me – you must – why did your parents place you with the Fathers and where did they go off after that? Did they ever come back for you, or at least keep in touch?"

"My father had done something that was not quite straight. Some embezzlement somewhere. The police were after him. The family had refused to bail him out. They left me at the orphanage – and – and– this the Fathers had let slip – killed themselves rather than go to prison."

O Molu of Bolu-Molu, O Kakima with her love of *phulka*s.

"I was rather small then – all this is what I picked up later—"

She saw Alex gape at her as she advanced towards him saying, "Papu, get me my Alice."

It took time for Alex to stop gaping. But then he rushed off and was back miraculously fast with the book – which she had won as a prize at school. Hardcover, pages edged in gold. Colour illustrations in profusion. And the name 'Kaushiki Gupta' on a red-bordered label as soon as one opened the book. Kushi ran affectionate fingers over it.

Childhood memories were recounted.

Tears fell and laughter rang out.

"But how?" Alex was still bewildered.

The letters were brought out and shared. The stunning revelation came. Apart from being a grand-aunt to Kushi, Minnie Tthamma was really grandmother to Alex. Uncle Molu had been her illegitimate child, with Portuguese blood in him, conceived in Chittagong though born and brought up in Kolkata by Tthamma as her own son.

Alex and Kushi sat by themselves till Tapen came in with the tickets. He had got tickets from the agency he knew and breathlessly proffered them.

Kushi took them but said under her breath, "I don't want to go."

She heard Tapen say, also under his breath, "Don't do this to me."

Alex was staring at them and Kushi covered up her spilling tears as those of joy at the discovery she had made. Tapen was duly taken aback. The conversation switched to quite another topic. Explanations were made and memories recounted yet again in the darkening balcony.

Rahul woke up to find himself endowed with a brother-in-law. He took it in with some amusement, and extended his invitation to come and visit them – any time they were back from Bangkok!

***

Kushi informed Veena of their news even while they were on the train to New Railway Station. There were so many things to be worked out with her. They collected Kuto from her on their way to their flat, and he clung to both by turns like a baby orangutan. But he had certainly been fine with Veena, and collected a pile of dinosaurs there as well.

The very next day they informed their landlord over the phone. They wanted to retain their flat at least for now. The Bangkok job was high-paying but fraught with uncertainties. The gentleman was okay with that and details were spelt out as to the *modus operandi* of the rent payment while they were away.

In between her packing, it occurred to Kushi to also inform the neighbour below of their imminent move to Bangkok.

When Kushi had made her quick decision to go to Rajpur, she had been away on one of her trips – or so Kushi had presumed. She went down and pressed the bell. She did not get any answer but could not afford to wait. Throughout the day she could overhear the bell go unanswered by whoever came pressing it.

Later in the evening, visitors going past the flat – and other residents too – paused before the flat and sniffed. They had sensed a stench wafting out of it. Hearing their voices, Kushi too went down.

The watchman had banged on the door with all his might but got no response. Kushi, nervous by now, suggested that they go up and shout down from her balcony which was just above the neighbour's. But even those cries had not got through.

The landlord was contacted. He came rushing with his set of duplicate keys. Meanwhile, the police had also been called in.

A swollen and stinking body had been found on the bed with a suicide note of sorts pinned to the *dupatta* primly covering the breast.

I am taking my last trip.

The bedcover was smooth. There were no signs of thrashing about in death throes – not even crumples. Her forehead had been equally smooth. An empty silver foil of sleeping pills was found on her bedside table along with an empty glass of water.

Kushi could picture her steps. Her neighbour had written a note, pinned it to the *dupatta*, taken her sleeping pills – all of them – and laid herself down on her bed – the single bed she had had for ever so long – spreading the *dupatta* on her thin breasts. Then she had gone –much further than Goa or anywhere the Nizamuddin Railway Station could take her to.

But as Rahul said, where was the time to be upset?

Kushi had to pack and leave the flat in some sort of order. Veena had done such a lot for her already. She could not call her in for the packing as well! Veena's solitary life was, after all, dedicated to loftier purposes like social work and incisive journalism.

Rahul had to join at Bangkok, a.s.a.p. So, both of them packed like mad. Sita too did her best though she was sad that they would be leaving.

The night before they were to leave, Rahul said, "Don't bother with cooking tonight." He ordered a huge pizza to be delivered at home. Somehow the pizza broke the spell of the last few days – the old places, the old people and the old Kushi. They were going to a new land and new life, felt Kushi. She was going to travel. Beyond the Indian subcontinent. Over the South China Sea.

As soon as Kuto had fallen asleep, Rahul began to make love right on the floor with its carpets rolled up. He pulled her down there and put pizza pieces from his mouth to hers. Kushi melted away in his warm embrace.

9

WANDERING NOWHERE

*I*t was a very different kind of bed from the bed she now lay in. How did she get to this platform of cold steel?

Kushi realized she could not stir, not to speak of getting up and walking away. No scream issued out of her mouth, gaping as it lay in shock.

What had happened? She couldn't be dead! But it did seem like that. How? Rape wounds? But she had died before the rape had taken place. It was, if anything murder and rape rather than rape and murder.

Will she go to hell now? Surely after what she had done, there will be no place for her in heaven! She hung in between, not knowing which route to take, completely lost as to the Devayana or the Route of the Deities.

She had wanted to travel but which was the *ayana* or route to take?

She remembered the college prayer which they had to say every day at the college assembly. Most of the students reached after it was over. She too had skipped it so many times. But she remembered its chant from the Vrihadaranyaka Upanishad:

Asato ma sadgamaya. Make me go from the transitory to the permanent,

Tamaso ma jyotirgamaya. Make me go from the dark to the radiant.

Mrityor ma amritam gamaya. Make me go from death to the deathless.

This final destination in the Vrihadaranyaka Upanishad was Brahmaloka and the way to it was through fire and sun and lightning. From there, there was no coming back, no spiralling down for those who can reach there. *Tesham na punaravritti.*

It was perfectly in tune with Brahmo thoughts. Rather, Brahmo thoughts were based on these tenets of the Upanishads.

But Kushi knew she was far from any such bright sunlit destination or even its fiery route. It was all grey around her, and vaporous. The winds were blowing her here and there, with no determinate direction. To Calcutta, Rajpur and East Delhi floated the cloud and was now blown to Kushi's five years in Bangkok.

10

BANGKOK

*I*ndeed, life had been nothing short of wonderful in Bangkok. The apartment allotted by Rahul's company was equipped with the most modern of gadgets and Kushi had found her housework light. Picking up Kuto was no problem either. There was school transport with excellent security arrangements at the entrance of their tall housing complex.

She was spellbound by the grand yet exquisite art the city displayed along with its modern technology. In some sense, Bangkok did not feel 'foreign' in the way U.K. or U.S.A. would have. She felt quite at home here. What is more, the weather was more like Kolkata than Delhi. The flora and fauna too. The Palash or Flame of the Forest burnt here as well, perhaps brighter.

Initially, Rahul had taken her around the principal tourist spots in Bangkok city. The *Phra Borom Maha Ratcha Wang* (Grand Palace), the various Wats or temples, the *Wat Phra Kaew* (Temple of the Emerald Buddha), the *Wat Pho* (Temple of the Reclining Buddha), the Chatuchak weekend market and even the Damnoen

Saduak Floating Market, the largest and oldest 'Floating Market' in Bangkok.

Later as his work in the office became even better paid and even more absorbing, he got her a car of her own, and Kushi learnt to drive. No, more than that, to venture out on her own in an unknown city.

Once Kushi had quite an adventure at the Floating Market.

She had stepped into one of the many narrow wooden boats which took tourists through a canal full of boats selling all sorts of local products – tropical fruits, vegetables and herbs, Thai dishes and handicrafts! Much bargaining was going on, in gestures and broken English. The boats came very close to one another for exchange but rarely crashed into one another. There were houses and buildings on either side, moving with the boats.

The boat Kushi had taken carried a group of tourists with a Thai guide who spoke English. Friendly and smiling, the guide was waving to all the boats to show their wares and bargaining in his own language on behalf of his group. His seat happened to be right beside hers.

Kushi bought a set of ten small key-rings – tiny straw dolls dressed in bits of colourful cloth. They were hooked onto a cardboard strip and covered by a strip of glossy paper. The others went in for the strips with small elephants hanging from the key-rings. There were none of those left for Kushi. The guide helped them in the bargaining and choosing, with the boat swaying all the while.

Kushi put her strip into the big shopping bag hanging by her arm. She bent over her purse for Thai Bahts. One Thai Baht was equal to 2.23 Indian Rupees.

Just then there was the sound of two boats knocking against each other – perhaps in their attempt to avoid another boat that seemed to be patrolling the canal. The guide had clutched at her bag to avoid canal water splashing over him. A tourist child had screamed. Then the slight mishap was over. The boat flowed smoothly again towards the pier.

Kushi had driven home and reached her flat by the lift.

But unloading her shopping bag, Kushi had found that her key-rings no longer had dolls hanging from them but elephants.

"Did I see wrong?" Kushi wondered, tired after the day. "No. They had been elephants I had taken." Anyway, how does it matter? The elephants are cute too.

They certainly were, with their tubby tummies and upraised trunks. But they were not what she had bought. Kushi frowned.

"I clearly remember putting the doll strip into my shoulder bag." She examined the elephant strip.

There was a call on the intercom from the security guard of their apartment. The guide at the Floating Market had come up here and wanted to have a word with her. Could he come up? Not thinking too much, Kushi answered, "Okay."

In about five minutes, the guide was up the lift. Kushi opened the door, still holding the strip of key-rings with elephants. He stood holding out the strip of key-rings with dolls – *her* strip.

"The one with the elephants?" He smiled in a friendly fashion. "May I have it? Has somehow got mixed up with yours when we hit that boat."

"No, it could not have done that 'somehow'," Kushi said slowly. "It could not have jumped out of my bag into yours. I had put it in deep."

The guide stopped smiling. "Give it to me, please."

"No. What's so special about that strip that you have come all this way to get it from me?" Kushi demanded.

"You just give it to me, Madam." He made a move to snatch the strip away from her hands.

"No," said Kushi.

The man lunged at them and in the scuffle, a key-ring got torn out of its strip. To prevent the man from taking it, Kushi stepped on it. She had not yet taken her shoes off and the heel of the right one pierced the elephant's tummy. Out spilt crushed, dry leaves of a kind she had never seen before.

Drugs!

The guide turned and quickly took the lift. Instead of trying to go after him, Kushi spoke on the intercom to stop him as he reached down. The security guards did it. The police too were on the scene in no time. It seemed that the Bangkok police was patrolling the Floating Market where narcotics were often traded in clever forms to foreign tourists.

"It's *kratom* leaves – still illegal although there are moves to remove it from the Narcotics Act," explained one of the policemen.

"*Mitragyana,* it is also called. Many people use it as a pain-killer or stimulant."

The young, friendly guide was into this racket, possibly for an extra bit of income. While taking tourists to the Floating Market, he smuggled this narcotic in the form of elephant-shaped key-rings where the elephants had been stuffed with *kratom* leaves by some other person or persons. That elephant was the mark of the supplier by which his product would be recognized in the foreign country to which it was being smuggled. On seeing a patrol boat approach, the guide had quickly exchanged his strip of elephants with Kushi's strip of dolls, taking advantage of the two boats knocking. If the patrolling police found the strip, it would be found in Kushi's shopping bag.

But it had been a false alarm and he had wanted it back. Fast.

The tourist group on the boat had contained one or two accomplices. That is why they had wanted only the elephants, not the dolls.

What an experience! Kushi was really overcome by it happening to her. But Rahul was not. He just heard it and made a casual remark like 'Wow', as though it was not of much interest to him, and turned to his laptop. Kushi had thought he might scold her for getting mixed up in all this, but he did not turn a hair.

Well, there was always Kuto to share it with, and then, electronically, Veena and Rakhi Didi.

"Glad that you are having such adventures," said Veena. "I miss Kuto though!"

Rakhi Didi said, "I am dying to visit you in Bangkok. Meanwhile, remember my tips, Kushi. Bangkok or not, you have to improve as a home-maker."

She had gone to the Grand Palace with Rahul. But to Wat Pho or the Temple of the Reclining Buddha, he said no at the last moment. His official work was getting heavier and heavier and the official lunches and dinners more and more numerous. When Rahul dropped out of a visit they had planned to Wat Pho, she decided to go there with only Kuto for company.

Buying a hand-crafted palm-leaf (How different from the Rajpur ones!), they had gone through the arch into yards dotted with small *stupa*s and huge porcelain pots with plants. The curved spires of long tiled roofs glinted in the tropical sun. Incense sticks filled the air with unknown aromas.

Under a huge shade, the golden figure lay in a restful recline, not a bit bothered by the continuous movement of visitors going around.

Its art was impressive, right down to the whorls in the black underside of the golden feet. But the very stillness of its mass was also remarkable. Clearly, it was in a position of penultimate rest, *pari-nirvana*. Kushi sat down with Kuto in a shady corner of the courtyard. She tried to tell her small son something about what he had been brought to see.

"Kuto, once upon a time, there was a prince named Siddhartha in a place named Kapilavastu in India."

"Near where we lived?"

"Not quite, but in India all right. His parents – the king and queen of Kapilavastu – loved him very much. They tried to keep him happy all the time. They did it a bit too much, I think. They did not let him see anything or anyone that could make him sad."

Kuto fanned himself. It was sunny and hot.

"But the world is full of many things that can make you sad. The king and the queen decided never to let Siddhartha see any of those things. Old people, poor people, sick people or dead people."

"How, Mamma?"

"By keeping him away from the world outside, within the palace of Kapilavastu." "In prison?" Kuto sounded interested.

"Oh no, Kuto. He had every freedom within the palace – every pleasure in life – and as he grew up, even a wife and a baby. Do you know what the baby was called? Rahul."

Kuto grinned, showing gaps in his teeth. Kushi went on. "But he never got a glimpse of the outside world. He was happy, but within the palace walls. He even had a chariot to take him around the palace gardens."

"On a conducted tour?" asked Kuto who had by then learnt that word.

"Sort of. Till one day he asked the charioteer to drive him out the palace grounds – through the palace gates. Well, he was the prince. The guard opened the gate. The charioteer drove him out. Outside, Siddhartha saw "Four Sights" as they are called

– an old man, a sick man, a dead man, and a man who had left home in search of the meaning of life. Siddhartha had never seen such people. He was shocked. Could there be such things in the world? Was the world full of old age, poverty, disease and death? Was there no way out?"

"Did he fight with his parents for keeping all this away from him?"

"No, he did not share with anyone how upset he was, not even with his wife. But he did not feel like staying in his palace any more. One night when his parents, his wife and his small son lay sleeping, Siddhartha left the palace."

"Just like that?"

"Just like that, and now I think we should make a move. I'll tell you the story on our way back."

After having Nom Yen, the pink, flavoured 'iced milk', they went home. Kushi resumed her story even as she drove.

"Once outside, Siddhartha wandered here and there. His only wish was to find out how people could be free of being poor, sick, old and dead. Finally, he came to a place called Gaya. He sat down under a big tree and began to meditate – that is, think of his purpose with his eyes closed." "Like a *rishi*?"

"Yes," Kushi tousled his head with her free hand. "Siddhartha ate nothing for days and months. He did not get up from his seat under the tree. His hair grew matted. His body grew thin. And he was not allowed to meditate in peace. It grew dark and stormy. Killer demons called Mara and Mari tried to disturb him in every way."

"By making faces at him? Baring their teeth?" Kuto bared his teeth with its budding canines (just like Papu did once! Kushi remembered).

"Sometimes even by becoming pretty dancing women tempting him to have fun with them. But Siddhartha never budged. He grew so thin that all his bones showed out of his skin. But he never got up. He said to himself, '*Ihasane shushyatu me shareeram* – let my body dry up here...'" Kushi recalled the line from *Nalaka* by Avanindranath Tagore which she had read long ago at school. She continued.

"Then one day he got an answer to his prayers. It lit up his mind –and he became the Buddha–one who had reached Bodhi or enlightenment. He opened his eyes slowly. The darkness and demons had vanished. It was a clear morning. Before him stood a village girl named Sujata. The Buddha broke his fast with the *payasa* or milk-rice she had brought."

"The same milk-rice that you make?" "Yes. It gave the Buddha the energy to get up and start on his way again. He did not want to keep his Bodhi to himself but wanted to share it with others. The *vriksha* or tree under which he had sat became known as Bodhi-*vriksha* and that spot as Bodha-Gaya. He began moving from the place to talk to people, to tell them what he had found out. People listened to him and followed him. These followers formed groups called Sanghas, collected alms, chanted prayers, and were very kind to people." "Did The Buddha ever go back home and see his baby?" Kuto asked.

"He did go to Kapilavastu, and share his message with Rahul who was a little bigger by then. Then he went on with his wanderings again. After more than forty years of spreading his wisdom, he reached a place named Kushinagar."

Kuto began to grin, and she was quick to add: "No, not a town named after me. Now listen. At Kushinagar, the Buddha ate some pork or mushroom that had gone bad. Eighty and weakened by food poisoning, he laid himself down, under two trees, reclining on his right side. That resting position is what we see in the Reclining Buddha statues."

"But then he did grow old and die?" said Kuto. "He had not found what he wanted – freedom from old age, sickness and death?"

"Well, he had found freedom from the fear or anxiety about them. We don't say that he died. We say he had got *pari-nirvana* or the complete end. That's the way to see the Reclining Buddha."

Kuto's eyes had begun to close. Home too was around the corner. Kushi had only a few minutes more to drive.

* * *

One day she had gone to a foot massage shop in an area known as Sukhumvit. She had heard so much about Thai massage!

In a congested alley, she found one which provided foot massage at the price she found reasonable. The shop looked a bit seedy but the young girls there were most pretty and gentle. A chant, possibly Buddhist, began to play and pleasantly warm water in a tub was brought in. There were flowers and herbs in the water and Kushi's eyes began to close as she leaned back on a chair, while delicate fingers raised her feet into the tub.

The chair had cracks in its rexin cover. The tub had patched-up leaks. It was a shabby little roadside shop she had entered. But perhaps because it was her first experience, Kushi found it out of this world.

The girl stroked her feet, sometimes pressing, sometimes pinching, and sometimes tickling them with the flowers. She droned on in broken English that this massage had come from Buddhist ideas and India. By then Kushi had gone into a state of utter relaxation, with all nerves loosening up. As the deft strokes grew faster, tears began to ooze out of her still-closed eyelids. This was bliss.

It was rude awaking to be asked for the payment and made to get up from the chair to make way for the next customer. Especially as she came home and found items missing from the shopping bag she had put down on the floor while hanging onto the purse.

She went to several more spas and became familiar with all the various massages they provided. But the first was the best.

※ ※ ※

Sometimes Rahul took her to his office parties. He had taken her to one or two in the early days of the marriage but not after Kuto had arrived. Here too he was a little reluctant. But Kuto was older now and Rahul was in a more senior position, that too in an overseas branch. Spouses were expected to join the parties. So that they could so without worrying about their responsibilities, kids too had their special space earmarked with twinkling balloons and smiling guards.

Kushi had never been more than pleasant-looking. Nor had she ever frequented beauty parlours. But she did wear her gorgeous silks on the occasions – the few she had packed in while coming. She did have a few eye-catching trinkets though, and she wore them along with some light make-up. The hotels where the parties were hosted were beyond anything she had ever been to in Delhi. The lighting and the music were enough to make her feel that it was heaven that she had entered.

The people there were a mix of Thai, Indonesian and Indian. There were a few from the West as well. Men and women were usually dressed formally, in the glossiest of black. The food, presented in between exquisite arrangements of orchids and flowers, was not just Thai but of all varieties, even Continental. The wine was a world in itself, beyond the few Kushi had ever tasted or even heard of. The wine glasses were works of art.

Kushi found the people friendly, trying to make an obviously Indian lady comfortable. Rahul, she thought, could have been more of a mixer. He stood in one corner, talking to a few specific colleagues, rather than introducing her to more, if not all. One of them was a particularly elegant Thai woman with laughter like a fountain from her slim body. Another was a white woman with straight silvery hair hanging in stark contrast to her black dress. Rahul was laughing and talking to them in utter oblivion of Kushi. Neither drawing her into their conversation nor conversing with her. Not even pouring her out some of the exotic drinks with their many colours. Kushi had her own ideas about courtesy but she did not let herself get hurt.

She herself was enormously thrilled. This was life.

On the drive home, Rahul made some rather rude comments.

"I wish you hadn't chewed your chicken so hard."

"Wine is to be sipped, not gulped."

"Learn to distinguish between a dinner plate and a dessert plate."

She did not pay much attention to them. That was Rahul's way. She was familiar with it by now.

As for the poisoned paddy fields of Rajpur, the trains going through the embankments, she had left them far behind.

❋❋❋

More than four years went by. Kushi and Rahul were at Pattaya Beach one Sunday morning. Kuto was with a Thai friend of his. He was taller now and well-adjusted to school life here.

It was Rahul who had suddenly proposed a drive to Pattaya, 100 km, that is, 62 miles south-east of Bangkok. A little surprised, Kushi had, of course, come along gladly.

In spite of the basic similarity between all sea beaches, the beach was breathtakingly lovely, curving spectacularly against the Gulf of Mexico, bringing 'Pattaya' or early monsoon wind blowing from south-west to north-east.

Apart from the scenic beauty, it also had history associated with it. It was here that in 1767 rebel Nai Klom had surrendered to the royal troops. A small fishing village till the 1960s, Pattaya had now become a popular tourist attraction with its high-rise buildings offering exciting entertainment.

After wetting his feet in the water a little – shoes carefully in hand– Rahul had sat down before a stall on the beach and begun on Thai Jasmine tea scented with lime. After spending some time gazing at a huge, bright balloon being floated across the bay, Kushi too had come back, and sat beside him,

She had taken her sunglasses off and put them on the table before them. Totally relaxed, she gazed at the sparkling oh-so-blue waters.

"Isn't it fantastic here?"

There was no instant response. Rahul kept squinting at the distance. Kushi's Nam Manao or iced-lime-with-sugar arrived on the table. Kushi took a sip and said, "Travelling had always been a dream of mine. Remember how I used to pester you to take me on your tours? Now you have fulfilled that dream of mine. I can send oodles of pics to Deepika with the two of us on the sea-beach."

Rahul was still looking into the sea. When he spoke, his voice seemed to come from across those waters. "About a couple of years back," his words were indistinct, "I met a girl."

"Yes?" Kushi frowned just a little. So what, she was wondering. Then came the thought –why hadn't he mentioned it before?

It all came out. It was incredible to Kushi. All she felt was numbness. Her throat went dry and she sipped her cold drink mechanically.

When it was all done, she just asked, "Have you told the girl how you feel about her?"

"It's mutual – the feelings," he said.

So, he did not even wait to tell her about it first – discuss its repercussions – been man-and-wife for one last time. Stunned though she was, she asked, "Well, what do you want to do about it now?"

"Why, marry her," she heard. She did.

"How?" Unconscious flippancy came into her reply. "Are you a 'bachelor boy'?"

To her shock, Rahul burst into tears, right then and there on the beach. A reflex reaction, she supposed. But he soon wiped away his tears angrily, saying, "I will get a divorce first, of course."

"Let the marriage be," Kushi cried. "I will make her my friend. You can go around with her. You can be with her all you want. But don't break the marriage up."

Her eyes stung. The glint of the sun upon the water became unbearable. The sunglasses she grabbed up did not help. Somehow, she got up and groped her way to the car.

For a few days, household life went on as usual. But the word had been said and the matter reared its head again. Rahul had presented her with air tickets for their return to India – to file a joint petition for divorce at a Sessions Court in Delhi. He had already contacted a lawyer there online and, if Kushi did not cooperate, he was ready to file singly.

The Bangkok flat with all its gadgets crashed about her.

11

EAST DELHI AGAIN

*W*ithin the week they were back in the trans-Yamuna flat that had been left vacant these last few years.

Kushi confided in Veena, breaking down as she did. "The first thing you do is send Kuto over to me for some days, and thrash the matter out with Rahul. Kuto is older now. You can't have your scenes before him. Have you got your maid coming?"

"No." Sita had moved. Anyway, Kushi had, in Bangkok, gotten out of the habit of having domestic help. Veena thought it a good thing. There would be no one to carry tales to neighbours.

"Fight it out with your husband now."

That is what Kushi had begun to do.

Only, she had grovelled rather than fought. She had hated herself for doing it but done it nevertheless. Using all the endearments she had for him, she had pleaded for herself.

For, she did not want later to have the feeling that she could have done more to save the marriage. "Give it another try. Whatever my faults, forgive me and let's start afresh!"

Rahul's face was set in hard lines. The passionate tears of Pattaya had crystallized by now into icicles. He meant business.

"You can't set the clock back."

He made it clear that whatever she said or did, he was "not going to budge."

"And what is to become of me? How will I live without you?"

"How should I know?" he had sneered.

"What about Kuto?"

"I can't think about Kuto now," he had answered with his fingers busy on his iPad.

There was a new neighbour downstairs. There was no question of confiding in her. Deepika, she knew, had of late begun to envy her. She could guess her excited comments, ringing with pleasure. No, no. Kushi could not share her news with her. After some thought, she rang up Rakhi Didi. She was in for a shock.

"Kushi, don't expect me to hold your hand. I had seen it coming. Hadn't I told you again and again to be more of a home-maker? To groom yourself better, to improve your cooking, and so on? Otherwise, your husband will run away from you. I knew Rahul would one day get impatient with your slovenly ways. Well, he's done it now. What is more, he has already told me about it – right after coming. Asking me not to be judgmental."

"Wha-what did you say?"

"I saw his point of view. 'Everyone has a right to be happy and I am not happy with Kushi – anymore.' Well, it's my principle as well. I have lived by it. You know I walked out of my first marriage. I gave Rahul his green signal immediately."

"You what?"

In the days of the landline, Kushi would have slammed the receiver down. Now all she could do was resolve never to ring up Rakhi again.

In a desperate moment, she even gave a call to her old professor, getting his number from the college. She felt that he would say something to help.

Professor Podder took some time to recognize her, but when he did, he patiently heard her through. Then he said, "So what's the big deal! Lots of women lose their husbands at your age. Get a job for yourself, and start afresh."

"But it's not so simple," she began.

"Look, don't waste my time or your own. You are getting a second chance at life – and you whine!"

What can one say to such a man! Kushi turned back to Veena.

"Look, you must see a lawyer at once."

"But Rahul has already been consulting one."

"For God's sake, don't sign anything that his lawyer drafts out for you. Get a lawyer of your own. That is also what your friend from

Rajpur thinks. Yes, I had his number. We have been in some sort of touch over industrial pollution issues. So, I rang him up."

"Oh," said Kushi. "You did? And what did Tapen say?"

"Ask Kushi to consult a lawyer once. Get her one. That's what he said. So, I *have* got you one. She's the best."

Kushi took her phone number and address down with numb fingers. Was this really happening to her? She tried for an appointment. It was in her private chamber in Gagan Vihar. Veena took her there. The walls were lined with thick books bound in leather and marked at the spines in red, black and gold. The chairs were rexin-bound and soft.

It was Veena who outlined the situation to the lawyer, a senior person with hard lines on her face. "Do you want him in prison for domestic violence?" she asked at the end of it. "Just tell me."

"But he hasn't beaten me or anything!" Kushi spoke out at last.

"That's all right. Mental cruelty is also domestic violence. I can file the 498A for you. He'll be behind bars."

"Oh, no. I don't want that. I love him," Kushi was frantic.

The lawyer made a face, if it could be respectfully said. Veena quelled Kushi with a glance.

"We'll get back to you, Ma'am. Your fees for today?"

Kushi had guessed by the décor of the chamber that the fees would be high. But at the sum mentioned, she blanched. She heard Veena ask for a possible concession, "You see, she's not working."

"I can get her interim maintenance by 498A but concession, no. The husband seems highly paid. She must pay me in full."

Veena paid for Kushi, but she admitted that this lawyer was well beyond her means as well. "I'll get you someone from a women's group I know."

The next day she directed Kushi to an address but did not come herself. For one thing, there was Kuto to keep occupied and entertained so that he did not ask too many questions about what was happening. Second, she felt that Kushi should jolly well articulate her own story. "D.I.Y. Start some time."

***

It was a D.D.A. flat in Mayur Vihar which Kushi reached by an auto. The buildings and streets of Bangkok had fallen far behind. The exotic palaces and temples had receded into the distance. She was back on the pavements of Jamnapar.

Climbing up the somewhat steep steps, she arrived at a second-floor flat. She was let into a bare room by a thin, simply-clad lady around fifty. It was obviously the sitting-cum-dining room of the flat, being used by a women's action group.

There was a placard nailed to one of the yellow-washed walls, with a slogan written on it.

Rona dhona ab karo khatam. Agey ki or badhao kadam. (No more tears. Ahead! With no fears.)

More placards stood rolled up in a corner. At the centre, there was a steel table and chair set, and a steel rack full of files. A few other women sat on faded plastic chairs that lay about the room. The lady took the steel chair and signed to Kushi to pull up one of the others. "Tell me everything, but without sniffling."

Kushi did so, as far as she could without sniffling.

"Hmm. Look at that woman over there, all hunched up. Her husband beat her up so bad that she cannot stand straight. It's difficult for her anymore to go on doing what she has been doing all her life. Sweeping and mopping and doing the dishes from house to house. Our organization has fought for the case. For free. That was because she was broken only in her body, not in spirit. Look at the other woman beside her. Speech-impaired. Raped by her husband's consent. She ran bleeding to us. We are fighting for her. Again, for free. There are countless cases like this everywhere. N.G.O.s like us take them up. You know why? Because they have in them the spirit to fight. No money, not much skill, not to speak of education. But they have spirit. The spirit to fight. Where's yours? What shall I fight with?"

Kushi saw her point and got up.

Veena got a little cross with her when she heard the story, from both ends because she knew this women's organization, although her own area of activism was child labour.

"I'll get you another lawyer. But you better put yourself clearly to him. What do you want as of now? Tell him that instead of rambling on."

This lawyer had his chamber by the side of Karkarduma Court, completed not so long ago, but already getting overcrowded. Young advocates had to share chambers. This one shared his chamber with two more, along with the shelves and alcoves stacked with files and court documents. It was afternoon but the Court smelt still of the sweat of the day. Kushi told her story again. As precisely as she could.

He seemed enthusiastic. "Ma'am, I can get you a good settlement but that is only if you let him go."

Kushi shook her head slowly.

"Thought not, from the way you told your story. You want to keep your man, right? Then you must get ready for a long, hard fight. *Aise lamba khinchunga ki dekhna*! (See how I keep this case dragging!)"

"But my husband has his job in Bangkok," Kushi began.

"That's to your advantage, isn't it? If he wants to keep it, he will also keep you. Coming for hearings to Karkarduma from Bangkok, how long can he do it? But meanwhile, give me all the dirt. Who is the woman? Do you have evidence of their affair? Do you have clippings of them together?"

No, Kushi did not. She did not even know who the woman was. Her brain was numb in this area. The pain was too much. It refused to work on questions such as: Was she that pretty Thai girl at the office party? Was it someone from his student days who has re-surfaced? She did not really want to know. He was going to leave *her* – how did it matter *for whom*?

The lawyer seemed disappointed that she did not have any 'dirt' to provide. "Well, you can always get it," he said after a while.

"How?"

"Set a detective on him – even now. I have a few numbers that I can get you. They know how to track him down to places he visits and numbers he calls – even international ones. They know the ropes. You'll have to pay through your nose, though."

Kushi did not discard this lawyer but her eyes were dull as she left the Karkarduma Court and went home. She dragged herself up and pressed the bell. Rahul, she knew, was at home. A streak of light could be seen under the door.

✻ ✻ ✻

Rahul opened the door but moved away as though in instant physical revulsion. He had been doing it of late. Childish as the act was, it hurt.

Nevertheless, Kushi followed him to the room where these last few days he had slept.

She wrapped her arms around his neck and tried to meet his lips. One last attempt at reconciliation she must make before the detectives were unleashed upon him. She must. She did. Rahul did not thrust her away. He stood still, stiff like a statue. Unmoving. Unmoved. Till her arms slackened and dropped down.

"*Sawb chole gyachhe.* It's all gone. All that I had for you," he said in an ice-cold voice. "Tomorrow I'll be gone too."

Then he picked up his phone and went to the balcony. "Fed up, I am just fed up. I am coming to you tomorrow."

Kushi had groped her way to her bed. It was not sleep but some sort of unconsciousness that had lashed upon her like a sea wave. But she got up from it as the sun pierced through the curtains to her eyes, and a faint creak of the opening door to her ears.

Yes, he was opening the front door and whether for the lawyer or for his lady-love, he was going out. Kushi got up and made it to the door, her sari unwinding behind her like her dignity, respect or pride. No. He was not yet gone. There was yet time.

She fell at his feet – upon his shoes, to be specific. "Don't go – don't leave me," she cried.

He jumped away.

It was a violent action– if not quite a kick.

"*Chhado*," he said. "I want out."

Kushi rose from the floor where his motion had flung her.

She caught hold of his shoulders and shook them. To and fro. Then, with her force rising to the beat of her heart, she flung him back. He was in the doorway and his head hit the edge at the corner where the wood met the wall.

After a surprised stare, he slid down silently. He did not get up. Blood from somewhere at the back of his head coursed down and spread out in a widening circle around him, reaching the *durrie* and the marble.

"Get up, Rahul!" Kushi tried to pull him up by his arms, to raise him up by the waist, and then fell upon his lips in an attempt to resuscitate although she had never learnt how.

His blood got onto her. It was still warm.

Then she too fell upon the floor, like the 'Love Lies Bleeding' bush in Minnie Tthamma's garden.

And then she screamed.

The door of the flat opposite opened, then that of the floor below – by its new occupant. The watchman came running. Then the neighbours.

"I killed him," Kushi kept screaming, with a hand upon her wildly thumping heart.

Someone called for an ambulance, someone else the police. A resident of the complex –a doctor – checked Rahul's pulse and made a wry face. A neighbour pulled Kushi up and seated her on the sofa, supporting her drooping body in her arms. The landlord came, pulling at his hair. Rahul was lifted on a stretcher and taken down to the ambulance that came. The police arrived.

Kushi simply said, "I shook him up too hard."

The hospital, it was learnt, had declared him 'brought dead'. After a few standard questions, she was taken into police custody. She cast a sweeping look at the flat – her home for many years with all its furniture, upholstery and knick-knacks. Her 'empire,' fallen to pieces.

Then a policewoman who had come picked up a scarf lying there and covered her face with it before she led her out. Kushi did not have to see the crowd that had gathered in the complex. Any way her eyes were unseeing, ears unhearing.

* * *

The lock-up was a new place Kushi travelled to. Veena came to visit her, lips pursed, going on with legal arrangements on behalf of Kushi. Kuto was at her place and Veena was tending to all his needs, psychological ones as well.

"Do you want me to bring him on my next visit?" she asked.

Kushi shook her head vehemently. She most emphatically did not want Kuto to see her through prison bars! Performing Rahul's last rites must have been enough of a trauma for Kuto.

Veena brought her pics and videos of Kuto on her phone whenever she came to see her in course of her judicial custody. But Kushi did not look at them. She felt she could not look him in the face after what she had done to him. Made all the dinosaurs extinct for him.

Veena told her that she had informed Tapen and a few others she could find contact numbers of.

But Kushi did not seem to hear her.

The lawyer Veena had engaged was the same as the one whom Kushi had met at Karkarduma upon Veena's reference. He wanted Kushi to suppress the fact of Rahul's demand for a divorce and make the whole thing appear as an accident. After all, the two of them had never had violent quarrels that had been overheard in the apartment complex and everyone there, including the landlord, remembered them as a happy couple with a son they both adored. Who other than Veena knew about Rahul actually leaving her? He could simply have been going on a tour – as he often did early in the morning. Old neighbours and the watchman could testify to that. But Kushi kept up her refrain of "I killed him," and the lawyer could not do much for her at the trial which took place at Karkarduma Court.

Rahul's announcement to leave her was taken as a 'sudden and grave provocation' and she was booked under Section 304 IPC and given the punishment for 'culpable homicide not amounting to murder'. It was clearly not a case of pre-meditated murder and, in the West, would have been regarded at the most as manslaughter. Kushi never changed her statement as to what had happened. Right from the start, she kept on her chant. "I killed him."

It was not a long trial.

The Additional Sessions Judge of the court sentenced her to imprisonment for ten years. Kushi did not let her lawyer appeal to the High Court. Her transition from an under-trial to a convict was simple and straight.

12

TIHAR YEARS

On entry into the prison in Tihar, Kushi's personal belongings were taken off and put away. The ear-studs, chain, wrist-watch and bangles of imitation gold that she wore were no problem to shed. But her gold-plated *loha* or iron bangle – the Bengali notification of having a husband – was difficult to take off because of the thin layer of fat she had put on in the years since her wedding when it had been slipped smoothly onto her wrist. Anyway, she had no right to it now. She was a widow. Besides, it was considered a potential weapon. She could perhaps hit her forehead with it and harm herself. The jailor called in a workman to cut it through. It was put away with other items of hers. How her professor had tried to impress upon her that it was a sign of slavery – a vestige of the past when a woman was captured and put in chains. How ironic that, for her, it was in a prison that it was taken off.

She was given a blue-bordered sari, taken to the Register Room where her name was written down in a register and then a small room – her cell. Zombie-like she went in and sat down on the bare floor provided with a *chatai*. Another woman was sitting there and looked curiously at her. The woman attendant who had brought her in locked the bars that formed the entrance or gate. She was now literally behind bars. A jailbird. Dadu had been in prison but for the 1942 freedom movement. She was here for killing her own husband! Ignominy.

Shabnam, the other women in the cell, seemed to be younger than her and had been there for some months. She was educated, articulate, and gave her tips on how to conduct herself in this vast prison complex.

Had the bars put an end to all her travels? It was not at all so, she discovered.

The jail had its own routine.

At around 6-30 a.m., attendance was taken. This being the female wing, there formed a line of women squatting outside their cells for a lukewarm cup of tea. Then they could go to the toilet by themselves but under supervision.

Now they had to go to 'work' –to the respective jobs they had been assigned. She had heard about Kiran Bedi's reforms and now she was part of it.

For female prisoners, it was the kitchen rather than the carpentry. Initially, she was assigned to the kitchen where the making of *vatata vada* became her specific task. She soon learnt to do it with speed. Division of Labour was practiced there, with the women taking turns at shredding the potatoes, boiling them, mashing them, shaping them and finally frying them in a huge cauldron. The *vada*s were then supplied to outlets at various courts.

Kushi had once gone to the High Court with Veena who was then fighting against a multinational's malpractices. In its precincts, and among the stalls for photocopies of legal documents, stationeries and snacks, there had been an outlet for *vada*s with a placard, *Made by Tihar Jail Inmates*. Kushi and Veena had munched them, admiring the Gulmohur blazing against the adjacent Purana Quila ramparts.

For all you know, Kushi's *vada*s could be making their way to outlets beyond. Her handiwork could be travelling instead of her.

The lunch provided at noon included *chapati, daal, sabzi* and some days a thin *raita*. Inmates, hungry after their physical exertions, usually fell upon it with gusto.

In the afternoons Kushi was assigned to a different task – making paper bags. It was not strenuous enough to make her keen for the dinner. But she had to go for it.

Once she came back to her cell, and spread her mat, on most days she had no trouble falling asleep. Dadu had taught her the rule, "Early to bed and early to rise". But waking up now cast her into a feeling of utter bewilderment. She felt like an astronaut ejected by his spacecraft into outer space. All around there were astral bodies, hurtling meteors, stars and planets. Rahul too was nowhere. Is it possible that he was not beside her to support her in this nothingness? Had she really killed him? But how?

Then after a few seconds, she came back to the solid reality of the prison cell, brick walls, the mat on the floor, and the open commode in the corner. Her eyes got acclimatized to the world that was still holding her close when the world she knew was all destroyed. This prison-cell. It was the *vivara* or hollow that Sita had asked the Earth Goddess for.

With this feeling surging in with her wakefulness, she faced the day. But the fear came next morning again and every next morning she had.

She never lamented her fate loudly like some other inmates did, loudly or otherwise. Once she had cried easily but now she was perfectly dry-eyed. Like Dimple Kapadia in *Rudali* singing '*Dil hum hum kare*,' she was at that stage where the heart was congested but the tear ducts were empty.

On some days she went spiralling down with her thoughts. Relentlessly they took her into a whirlpool, a cesspit, rather. What she then did was roll over to the back of the cell, cocooned by her *chatai*. Getting as close as she could to the wall, she tried to dig her nails into its plane surface as if to embrace it. But wasn't it a wall that had killed Rahul? More than her flinging him back after shaking him up? She recoiled for a moment from the wall then flung herself on it repeatedly. She felt the very bones in her skull rattle and her forehead swell up.

The other woman in her cell saw her but could not control her frenzy. She called for the attendants. They opened the cell, got in and pulled Kushi back from the wall.

"*Yeh to sir patak kar marne ka kaushish mein thi.* (This one was trying to crack her own skull and die)." That was the report.

But Kushi knew that she had not really wanted to die – but only to feel what Rahul had felt – as if to unite with him in pain. Suicide was not in her mind, as far as she knew! But how else to meet Rahul again?

The first aid brought the swelling down, and Kushi became calm again. She was taken to the counselling facility of the cell. The therapist, a middle-aged lady, brisk and competent, talked to her a couple of times, and recommended, "Cry and let it all out."

She needed to, for her mental health. There were instructions. "Sit in a corner of the cell facing the wall. Make yourself feel bad. Think of what you had done. Think of where you have descended to. Think of what or whom you are missing. Slowly you will find your chest tighten, your throat hurt, nostrils flare and eyes fill. Tears will threaten to spill. Let them. Do not force them back."

But her lacrimal glands just did not respond to the therapist's prescription. There was no relief for Kushi in tears.

Till a day came when she had unexpected visitors. Tapen and Papu all the way from Rajpur. Veena had been updating Tapen who had been updating Papu. They had taken some time, but now they had come. They had put up in a small hotel beside the New Delhi Railway Station, met Veena and Kuto, and with directions from Veena, come to look Kushi up.

There they stood in some sort of visitor's room, also barred.

"My fault, Kush, that I ever let you go," Tapen said huskily.

Then it happened exactly as the therapist had said. Her chest tightened, throat hurt, nostrils flared and eyes filled. Kushi tried to send her tears back but they rushed out of her eyes, snot soon bubbling out of her nostrils. Tapen kept quiet but she heard Papu say, "Didi, we'll take you away as soon as you are free. There's work there in the villages – for you to do – standing alongside us."

Kushi raised her head and wiped her nose. She learnt that Mashima–Tapen's mother – had passed away (partly why he could not come earlier) and that Papu was now married – to Neera – in an inter-faith marriage whose approval in the village was won largely by Tapen (also partly why he was late).

Neera had wanted to come along but Tapen and Papu had not let her. She was expecting and the delivery date was near. Kushi's eyes shone through their tears. The child would carry her own family line forward and would be her own nephew and Kuto's cousin, even if only a few came to know it. But poor Mashima had not acquired her *bou*. Tapen was hers. A faint smile came to the corner of her lips.

"Jalpa and Jhumri?"

"Taking care of Neera just now, along with the house. Only, they just don't believe that this could happen to you!"

"It was a good idea of yours," said Tapen, "to formally gift the house away to Alex soon after going to Bangkok."

It had been a long, expensive and complicated process executed through a 'power of attorney' but Kushi had insisted on it and Rahul had provided every cooperation.

Yes, now it was no longer an empty house, resonating with crickets at night. It was a home to young people, working, living and loving together and creating new life between them. Soon it would ring out with a baby's cries, chortles, pattering feet and prattling voice. And they would be those of Minnie Tthamma's own great-grandson! Would she know as she hovered in the morning among her flowers and butterflies?

✸ ✸ ✸

After that visit, Kushi settled down better into prison life.

She got to know her cellmate Shabnam better. A spindly girl, much younger than Kushi, she was a university student who had been picked up on the pretext of being associated with some terrorist group. She had ever since then been awaiting a trial where she could at least have an opportunity to speak for herself. But it seemed as if she was already serving a sentence!

She sometimes recalled her earlier days with cheerfulness. "Jantar Mantar was usually where we squatted after marching with our banners and shouting '*Murdabad*' and '*Hai hai*'. Such fun it was!"

"Fun?"

"To protest against injustice is itself an exhilarating experience," she pressed the boiled potatoes with force. "Whether you get justice or not, you get freedom from your shackles."

She shared that *Animal Farm* was the first book she had read completely on her own, taking it to be a children's story about animals. It had compelled her to take up *The Communist Manifesto*. She was a changed person by the time she came to the call 'Workers of the world, unite! You have nothing to lose but your chains!'

"Was it only the books," Kushi asked, "or some leader as well?"

For a second, Shabnam's hands paused on the mashed potatoes. "The President of our Students' Union, a Law student. He explained Marxism to me further – the concepts of crisis and revolution, socialism and communism."

"You know, I have always wondered – what is the difference between the two – socialism and communism? Why have two separate terms – for what seems to me the same?"

Shabnam was eager to explain. "No, no. They are not quite the same. Communism is an advanced form of socialism – the ultimate of the 'modes of production' that Marx defined – primitive communism, slavery, feudalism, capitalism, socialism and communism."

Not quite following, Kushi looked at her bright, shining face so as to say, "Go on."

"You will find it in *On Economic Inequality* by Amartya Sen. Beautifully explained with a quote from Marx. Socialism is the economic system that emerges out of capitalism and still carries some of its mentality. Distribution is still according to individual productivity or 'deeds'. With time, self-interest no longer is the main reason for productive activity; distributive activity too can be social. Society can write on its banners 'From each according to his abilities, to each according to his needs'. People can be free in the full sense of the term. That's Communism."

"You believe in that state? – I mean, you believe that it will actually come some day?"

"Of course! It used to be there, in the Primitive Community form of society. It can still be found in tribal societies."

Kushi remembered the dance in honour of Lugubudu. Dancing, not performing. Holding hands, not racing against one another. No solo dancers have risen to fame from tribal societies.

But then Kushi was also reminded of the portrait on the ground floor of their house in Calcutta. No slaves, no masters. Wasn't that too an affirmation of faith in liberty, equality and fraternity?

Aloud she asked, couldn't help doing so, "Where's your *guru* now?"

"In a corporate job, by dint of an arranged marriage!" Shabnam's smile was twisted. "But there are always others, you know, those who do not betray the cause. In this very jail now, in the men's wing, there is one such. Going to the gallows, I am sure, but standing by his beliefs."

Kushi nodded. She knew, like most others, whom Shabnam meant.

✳ ✳ ✳

The jail had a library and inmates could issue a book or two into their cells. After her talk with Shabnam, Kushi began to use this facility oftener. There was so much she had missed in terms of education in her desire to be with Rahul and set up a home with him. She could have done her Master's course and gone in for even higher education. Even an erudite scholar like Professor Podder had considered her bright enough to remember. Mr Chatterji had found her services useful. Rahul posing as Amit had found that she had her own views on contemporary issues.

At the same time, there had never been a rebel in her. How nervous she had been about going to school, how anxious for getting all her sums right. She had been a good little girl, content with taking walks with her grandfather instead of running around with friends in the playground. Never bawling when her father left Calcutta for extended periods in Rajpur, never fretting for her mother when she went to join him. Her single act of violence had been to *keep* her husband rather than to break free from bondage.

So, when warders referred to Kushi as an inmate on 'good behaviour,' she was not 'on' any kind of behaviour, other than her natural.

"Actually, you are so good that…" Rahul had said one night in a tone as if of reproach.

"That what?"

But he had left the sentence incomplete.

Had Kushi been docile to the extent of being boring? The Thai colleague whom Kushi had seen at the party had seemed intoxicating like Champagne. But hadn't Rahul always wanted, a stay-at-home wife, a *gharer bou*? A *grihalakshmi* to be always there to open the door when he came back from tours?

But was that really what Rahul had wanted? Docility? Obedience? Subservience? Why then had he taken to Rakhi Didi such a lot?

And that night while driving back from the party, why had he commented about his colleague – more to himself than to Kushi, "Whatever she feels, she says it straight, and does not cower before the boss. She's spunky." Was it that quality which drew him to her?

Approaching middle age, had he been knocked off his feet when at last faced with what he had always wanted but without knowing? Or was it simply the appeal of younger flesh and exotic looks? After all, in the last couple of years, Kushi had put on a little weight. But didn't most wives do so? But, no. It probably was not that.

At some point in the last few days, he had said it was not a physical attraction that was drawing him away. It was a call from soul to soul. She smiled bitterly the next moment, remembering how he had rejected her physical overtures the last night he – or they – ever had. Soul had obviously been calling.

Let me go.

Rahul's cry still rang in her ears. She had always agreed to whatever he said –given in – conceded –even been a doormat. But this plea of his, how could she give in to!

"Rahul, I am close to my forties. You desert me now? I have given away my entire youth for you!"

"What about the youth I have given up for you? I have thrown away happiness with both my hands! Let me at least have the years I can still have! I am at the fag end of life and everybody has the right to be happy."

"But didn't you get any happiness from me in all these years?"

"Oh, those scraps of happiness! If you only knew what a pain in the neck you have been!"

"But what was it? What had I done – rather, what was it that I had *not* done – for you?"

"You just didn't have it – that zing – that kick in life which I wanted. You were a deadweight round my neck – an Albatross I had shot down."

Kushi knew that poem by Coleridge – *The Ancient Mariner*.

So, she had become that to Rahul – how and since when? Since he came here, met this Thai colleague and discovered how good life can still be?

An earlier incident came back to her. They had gone to visit an acquaintance. Throughout, the wife there had been scolding the husband.

"This man here knows nothing but his job!"

"Come on, lazy lump, give me a hand in laying out the table!"

"When are you taking me to see a film?"

"Useless he is, when choosing vegetables or fruits!"

The husband made no protest but merely smiled.

While coming back, Kushi had teasingly said to Rahul, "Did you see, how that Mrs Chaube was scolding her husband? Do I ever scold you like that?"

Pat had come the reply from the driver's seat, "Sure, you don't say much. But when you do, it is a whiplash."

But what had she ever said to Rahul that had hit him so badly? She had been brought up to be polite and gentle in her speech. Where she had gone wrong? She never knew.

They hardly quarrelled and even if they did, they made up pretty soon. They had a special way of doing it. Not holding one's hand to the other, but just one finger. If the finger was taken, the rest of it followed. If it was not, one waited some more time and proffered it again. If the other proffered a finger on his or her own, one just took it. It was a quaint way, special to themselves.

With this remembrance, it seemed that a whiff of the smell of Rahul's hair floated into her cell. The one he had when he came from a foreign tour. O Rahul, Rahul.

❋ ❋ ❋

One after another, the memories reared their heads as in *Absent in the Spring* by Agatha Christie who too had experienced a divorce trauma.

Rahul had always been fond of good clothes, bright-coloured shirts for example. Even scarves around the neck. Shoes and boots well-polished. Clothes that drew attention to him. He had carried them well. Everything looked good on him. Kushi had often told him that.

So proud she had been of his looks that she had not bothered much with her own. She did not usually wear ornaments, except when going out with Rahul which had not been so frequent! Only a thin gold chain, ear-studs and bangles. The coral and conch-shell ones had been kept aside with time but the gold-bound iron bangle she had continued to wear. If she accompanied Rahul to some party, she sometimes wore the jewellery he had occasionally given her as presents. She could never snap the bracelets shut by herself. Rahul had to do it for her and that's what she had loved. Deep inside perhaps it was the upbringing she had received from her grandparents, principled and *khadi*-clad. But it was more the feeling that she was loved – by Rahul – for herself –as she was – and there was no need to further prettify herself.

In the process, she had reduced herself to a dull, dowdy, stay-at-home wife, a domestic drudge who wasn't even good at her job. Was it this that had made Rahul wants to chuck her out and begin afresh? Or even earlier – never take her along on any tour – be free of her at least for those days?

"Take better care of yourself and your home," Rakhi Didi had said. "Otherwise, your husband will leave you and run away. He is already impatient with your ways. I have seen it in his face."

Should she have paid more attention to Rakhi Didi's admonitions? But whenever she had tried, hadn't he said, "Remain you as you are."

There had been the matter of her culinary deficiencies.

She had to admit that she had not been much of a cook. Yes, Rahul had drawn attention to it right after their marriage. Coming back from dinner at some colleague's place, he had remarked, "Did you see how crisp their rice was?" It was a reference to the fact that her own rice was often a bit lumpy – with grains sticking to one another.

But surely that wasn't such an important matter? Besides, it was not that Rahul cribbed about food constantly. Mostly he seemed quite content with what was served to him at the table. He was, or so Kushi had thought, so engrossed with his job, so absorbed in his career, that food did not matter all that much to him. Anyway, he was always getting the best of food in his official lunches and dinners, often held in Mariott, Hilton and even Neemrana.

And he often ordered Chinese and Italian home, to be eaten while lolling on the floor. Kuto loved spreading out a little folding table on the floor for those home deliveries.

No, Kushi had not been aware of any great grievance in the way she had run her home. She had gone about thinking she was doing okay. Rahul had let her do so. Let her fall into a rut while he climbed higher and higher? Why? Because somewhere along that career path with an ever-increasing gradient, Rahul had decided to get rid of her.

To replace rather than reform.

That would explain his comment, "The stuff that you have been serving me all these years, have I ever said a word about it?"

Naturally not. One does not try to improve the work of a maid or nanny whom one has decided to sack at the end of the month.

Years of loyalty had been of no account. He "wanted out", as he said. Create a new life with a new wife. Nothing that Kushi said or could do would have made a difference to him. Not even the fact that Kushi was the mother of his son? What had been lacking in her that even Kuto could not compensate for?

No. As he said, he "would not budge".

Somehow, who 'the other woman' was still did not bother her too much. She did not matter. She was 'not-A' to her being 'A'. She was all that she was not; she had everything she did not have. Okay. She did not torture herself too much with questions like how they had met, how their mutual feelings had developed and found expression, and lastly, how she had taken Rahul's loss. None of this was in her 'universe of discourse.' For her, she was not just an unknown entity. She just did not exist.

But Rahul did.

***

It was the new activity she was assigned that saved her from sinking into the abyss of remembering Rahul, of analysing the past where he was alive, re-analysing it *ad nauseam.*

Shabnam had revived Kushi's interest in books and she began to frequent the jail library and issued books from there to her cell. Beginning with some Marx under Shabnam's guidance, she soon diversified into social history and even contemporary fiction – as available there.

Observing this, the prison authorities moved Kushi more into the library to assist with its book accession process and the ongoing Saksharata Abhiyan or Literacy Drive. It suited her much better.

Together with Shabnam (incredibly, still around as an undertrial), she began to take the literacy drive forward within the jail. Most of the women inside were illiterate or just a little better. A few women had been pregnant at the time of their indictment, and their kids had been born in the jail. Kushi and Shabnam introduced them to the Hindi alphabet and then to retold or abridged works of literature. The response was encouraging. For, the women, though neo-literates, identified themselves with adult themes rather than lessons in elementary textbooks. One of them was Chinmoyee or Chinu as she preferred to be called. She reminded Kushi a little of Jhumri.

"Kushi Didi, what's the use of an alphabet book with things we don't have dealings with? A for Anaar. How many of us get to eat an *anaar*? Ang for Angoor. Well, I haven't tasted one myself."

"She has a point," said Shabnam. "Only Communism can get rid of this elitist bias that starts with the very alphabet."

"Perhaps we may try," said Kushi.

"How will you market it," said Shabnam, "even if you write it?"

"We can try it out here, and then reach out to some N.G.O. My friend Veena can help in networking."

Kushi began on it, in her mind.

A se Ab

A se Azad

Ab man mein me lao zor

Azadi ke chalo ore

No, not this perhaps. But something along these lines? They could all think about it and pool their ideas.

Chinu had killed her own daughter, a newborn girl-child. Kushi had at first recoiled in horror. But Chinu had not looked abashed at all. She already had three daughters and her in-laws, not excluding the male members, had said that they would throw her out if she had one again.

"Stuffed salt into her mouth while breastfeeding her…Had the other three to take care of."

"Why hadn't you got rid of it earlier?" asked Shabnam.

"We hadn't known."

"You could have gone for a test, even though it is illegal."

"We did. But it's *gair-kanuni*, as you said. So, the clinics want *rishwat*. My in-laws didn't have enough."

"So you had to carry it through to find out?" Kushi was aghast.

"Even then they called the police and showed the dead baby on my lap with salt sticking to her mouth."

"Why was that, to save themselves?"

"To get rid of me anyway. They had a second marriage already finalized for my husband. He was himself keen on it."

"What has happened to your other three?"

"How do I know, Shabnam Didi? Has anyone looked me up in the jail?"

Kushi found herself saying, "We'll write out a new alphabet book together. You will tell me the words, and I will make the rhymes."

She wondered whom she was comforting, Chinu or herself.

* * *

Days, months and years went by.

Despite Veena's suggestions endorsed by the lawyer (whose practice has grown, as Veena informed her), she stood firm on her resolution never to try for parole or appeal to the High Court for a reduction of the sentence.

She wanted no temporary respite. She wanted to serve out her sentence. She wanted to pay her dues in full. And then get her full freedom.

"How will I live without you?" she had once cried to Rahul. "*Ami tar ki jani*! How do I know!" He had answered. Well, here she was doing it.

In fact, she was beginning to get quite attuned to it. Even gaining weight along with a few wisps of grey hair. She was not tortured by any feeling of confinement. She felt even a sense of security here. What did the world outside hold for her, anyway? It did not contain Rahul. As for Kuto, he had taken his SAT and gone to the United States. Veena had been mother enough for him. She had pressed Kushi to meet him once before he left. But Kushi had stood firm. She just did not want Kuto to see her like this.

But she had written him a letter with writing material from the jail. She remembered her father showing her a letter stamped 'Alipore

Central Jail'. It was from her grandfather to his two sons when he had been imprisoned for joining the Non-Cooperation Movement. Kushi's father had preserved it as an inspirational message. Would Kuto do the same, for a mother serving a prison sentence for homicide not amounting to murder, that too, of his father?

Still, she wrote:

Kuto, my Kuto, I can't tell you how happy I am that you are going to the States after getting admission to Arkansas University. You will be going even further away from me, and all you have known so far. But I take it as a cause for celebration, even and especially for me. You know, I have always wanted to travel, to see the world. But I had wanted to do it with someone – with Daddy ever since he came into my life and I set up a home with him. I have broken up that home – which was yours too. Taken the roof from over your head in one act that I had not intended. Made you an orphan twice over. Mea culpa.

That is why, I let you go – with elation in my heart. I could not do that for Daddy when he pleaded with me to 'let go' of him. I wanted to remain a pain in the neck, an Albatross choking him. I forgot what my grandfather had tried to teach me. Tena tyaktena bhunjithah. Enjoy it by relinquishing it.

People will sometimes tell you to come back from abroad and take care of me. They will tell you that it is your foremost duty. I tell you, don't.

Stay there and make the most of your opportunities. Settle down there if you can, but more importantly, see the world. Travel. Whatever happens to me, you are not to come back to take care of your own old mother, alone and helpless, as others will phrase me. You are to fulfil yourself and go places. Your father would have gone from peak to peak – if I had let him. He too wanted to travel – only he did not mind if it was with or without me. Your travelling will unite us. For, I will always be with you, rather, in you. Seeing with your eyes all that I ever wanted to see.

"Pretty soppy," commented Veena as she took the letter after the jail formalities. "Anyway, I will give it to him. I will go now. Have to do a lot of things to do for him. Getting proper woollens and starting the packing."

Did Kushi feel a tiny pang? Wasn't it for her to do things for her son? Hadn't she once bought his backpack and water bottle?

The next time, informing her of Kuto's reaching safely, Veena mentioned that she would now look for some small flat in Dwaraka, a fast-growing suburb on the western edge of Delhi. The N.G.O. that she was attached to was extending there, and getting some international recognition as well. "I am also going West!" she joked.

The other news was that Giten Dada and Rakhi Didi had located Veena through Facebook and inquired after Kushi. They were still at Ranchi, and together. Only Rakhi Didi has been so badly struck with gout that her travels had been severely curtailed. Daughter Tuktuki was working in Ranchi itself.

They had sent Kushi their love and said that the moment Kushi was released, she was to visit them in Ranchi.

Would she?

Shabnam sometimes asked her, "What do you plan to do once you are out? It's not all that far off. Think it out now. Or then you won't know what to do."

In a travesty of justice, she was still an undertrial and had lost all her youthful looks just by waiting.

She had a point, but Kushi simply didn't think of the time she would be free. It was not of much interest to her. No, even more. It held a kind of fear for her. She did not know what it was like – now that Rahul was no longer in it.

Veena, she was sure, would be there when she got released. She would take her up in her Maruti and drive her to her place, Dwaraka by that time. She would have a good bath and eat at a table. Then they would decide what Kushi could do. She would, of course, have to work for a living. But she was confident that she would find something somewhere. She could join the women's organization she had once visited, help in secretarial work, teach neo-literate women or actually fight for them. Oh, there was a lot of work that could be done in Delhi itself. Why hadn't she ever looked around and found them?

Or she could go back to Rajpur and join Tapen in his work of rural uplift. That was always there, like Tapen himself. Without fuss, but at hand. She knew she could always count on him. And, Alex, her own Papu, with Neera and the kid. Jalpa and Jhumri would be there too.

That was Alice's Wonderland. Waiting for her.

But for now, there were the walls of Tihar Jail around her. She remembered another line from the *Gita* that Dadu often chanted. '*Yatha niyuktosmi tatha karomi.*' As I am placed, so shall I serve.

For the last few days most inmates had known that an execution was about to take place but nobody knew exactly. The mercy petition had been rejected by the President of India and the news had reached the women's wing as well. Being early February, it was still very cold in Delhi. At around 7-30 a.m., surprised attendants saw two doctors and a *maulavi*, obviously by arrangement, arrive at the jail. Wiping their eyes, they later told those in the women's wing that when the man in his high-security solitary cell was informed, he was calm and only wanted to write a letter to his wife. After his prayers, he was offered tea, and once he had finished it, asked for more. As he was being taken to the gallows, he greeted the jail staff familiar to him by their first names. "Hope you will not hurt me," he said to the executioner.

He was buried inside the jail complex, to prevent any unrest outside.

A red-eyed Shabnam said, "He was only forty-three."

Kushi shuddered. Rahul too had been forty-three when 'executed' by her. Unintentionally but unfairly nevertheless.

It was right not to have appealed for parole or a reduction of sentence.

13

TIHAR TO ALWAR

So, it was somewhat of a shock when she heard through the lawyer that he had got her a release – a little ahead of her term – citing her 'good conduct.'

He had not only filled out in girth but also developed a certain authority of manner. Kushi realized that her release was a fact accomplished. He had done something at last for his client.

The only problem, he said, was that 'Veena Madam' could not be informed. She was abroad somewhere, attending an international seminar on child labour. He offered to send his 'junior' to pick her up tomorrow when Kushi would be released.

Kushi declined politely. She did not want to begin her new life with unnecessary favours. She was sure that she would be able to manage on her own.

It was strange to get out of prison clothes and into a set of clothes she hardly recognized. Washed and pressed, they were still the ones she was wearing when she had been taken into police custody. The broken iron bangle with gold plating was also returned, along with her earstuds, bangles, watch and chain– all gold plated. They still had a shine on them. She tied them up loosely in a faded scarf that had also been there among her items.

She was also given whatever she had earnt by her labour at the minimum wage rate.

Such earnings are often arranged to be sent to the accounts of any dependents of the inmate concerned. But Veena had never agreed to any such arrangement. She had seen to it that Rahul's money was put in a trust for Kuto, the interest of which would be sufficient to finance his education and upkeep till the time he came of age. "And I am there, am I not, his Ma-si?"

So, there was a tidy bit that Kushi was handed over as she was released. The inmates, led by Shabnam, tearfully gave her a *jhola* with 'Made at Tihar Jail' woven into it.

Stepping out of the jail, she did not know where to go or even where to look. Janakpuri stretched all around, busy and congested, teeming with life. Vehicles going by were the first to catch her bewildered eyes. Auto-rickshaws, bikes, cars, buses and trucks. So much movement from so many! What model of Maruti was that? She took a few steps forward. Which flyover was this? And was that huge silverfish, a metro train, started in Delhi only after she had gone to prison?

She took a few steps ahead and realized the value of Shabnam's advice to plan what she would do once she was released. She had never envisaged the possibility of Veena not being there to pick her up. Her last day at the jail had passed too quickly to plan.

What to do now!

She took a few more steps, all her possessions in the *jhola* hanging from her right shoulder. A bike went hurtling past and she jumped back in fear of being run over. The noise of the passing vehicles was also terrifying. In the slow pace of life within walls, she had forgotten the rush of life outside.

An auto slowed down before her, obviously looking for a passenger. Without much thinking, she got on to it.

She decided not to go to East Delhi. No Jamnapar just now, especially with Veena not there. She made the auto drive her to South Delhi. And then a great sense of exaltation came over her. She was on the move! She was travelling! This was what she had always wanted, and now she was doing it again! The world was at her feet and it was moving too! Chanakya Puri with mauve Jarul on the roundabouts, Niti Marg, Shanti Path, and Satya Marg followed, with borders of Canna or Indian Shot.

The Embassies, the Railway Museum, the Vet Hospital and V.I.P. vehicles speeding past.

Exhilaratingly different from the prison atmosphere where she had spent almost a decade of her life. Yes, it was good to be out. To be free. So what if there was no Rahul beside her!

A quieter stretch, Shantiniketan. Then Vasant Enclave and I.I.T. Gate when the roads were crowded again.

The auto-walla arched his neck and wanted to know where exactly she wanted to go. How much more was he to drive! But Kushi did not want him to stop – anywhere at all. She just said a name that came to her head. 'Munirka'! Actually, she was not familiar with the lay of the land in South Delhi. She had lived in

East Delhi, that too mostly within the apartment complex. It was either Rahul or Veena with whom she had gone out. This was a new experience for her. Intoxicating.

She lost all sense of hunger and thirst and of time and distance. Her hair flew around her face.

She did not get down even at Munirka. She made the auto turn to J.N.U., Vasant Kunj, Mahipalpur, and then towards the Delhi-Jaipur Highway or the National Highway 48.

But beyond a point, the auto refused to go. It did not have an N.C.R. permit and was on the brink of the Delhi-Haryana border – the Kapashera Border. Kushi paid him as he stared at her as if she was a madwoman. She looked around. There was a small shop hung with streamers of shampoo sachets, tobacco pouches and potato chips packets. The shop also had a counter with big biscuits, obviously homemade, cough-drops in jars and cold drinks in open plastic cartons. Kushi had a Limca – after ages. It was so good that she had another. She suddenly remembered the one at the prison who, after drinking one cup of tea before being hanged, had asked for one more. Had he got it? She did not know. But she could have her second Limca. This was being alive. This was being free.

※ ※ ※

She saw that there was a 'garage' or repair shop around the corner. Several cars were lined up, the owners calling for attention from the already busy workers.

There was also a *kali-peeli* taxi standing.

It brought the memory of the taxi in the garage of the Calcutta house – and a sense of security born of life's first impressions.

She went and hired it on the spur of the moment.

"*Kahan jana?* (Where to?)" The driver asked.

"*Zara ghoomne,* (Just for a drive)," she replied.

She too would travel – like Rakhi Didi, like her neighbour downstairs – all by herself.

"*Kuchh to bataiye?* (Say something at least?)" the driver pressed.

"Neemrana," she said, she did not know why. She did not even know where exactly it was, or how far.

The name came out from some recess of her memory. A hilltop fort of the 15th century, the first fort in Rajasthan on the way from Gurgaon. Whoever had been there had praised its ambience. One could even book an overnight stay there, it had been said.

Rahul had once attended a seminar there but never taken her along…

The details were hazy but the hurt was still there.

Well, now she would go there herself. Come back if there was no room available, but at least go to mark the day of emancipation.

"Neemrana," she said again.

The taxi-driver looked at her a little quizzically and asked, "*Akeli ho?* (Travelling alone)?"

She nodded and without any bargaining about the fare he asked for, jumped in. Her *jhola* scattered its rupees across the back seat.

She made no haste in picking them up. The man himself leaned over from the driver's seat, gathered some of them and handed them to her. He picked up the ornaments as well, which had fallen out of the folds of the faded scarf. His hair brushed against her breasts for a moment but she thought nothing of it. The car started on its way with a sound that showed that its silencer needed repair.

Soon it was on the National Highway 48 and speeding off along it.

Gurgaon came and went. The hills of Manesar approached. Small villages appeared on either side, separated by stretches of fields and bushes. Trucks and smaller vehicles were speeding along. On either side lay green and yellow fields, bringing back memories of Rajpur. The rides with Tapen and Papu. Well, she will contact them soon. Just now, this was fine. The sensation of being all by oneself but at liberty.

The road signs pointed towards Jaipur. Hills emerged, some close enough to see white-washed temples on their green-brown bodies, some blue-grey in the distance.

The driver had a small cell phone with him. Once or twice, he brought it out and spoke to someone softly. Kushi wondered if she should borrow it and try some numbers half-remembered. But no, she wanted to enjoy these hours alone. They would never come back.

*Dhaba*s too cropped up on the roadside, usually two or three together. The sun began to dip. The taxi pulled up beside a *dhaba*. The driver got down and brought her a cup of tea as she sat inside looking out of the window. He settled down at one of the tables in front of the *dhaba* with a cup for himself. She saw a man from another table join him. They fell into a chat, and she saw the two look at her often. But then her eyes began to close. The evening light was soothing, and she would soon be in Neemrana.

There must be hotels on the side of the highway even before one got to the fort at the top of the hill. She would find a room for herself for the night – in case it had closed its gates by the time she reached. Tomorrow she would go up to the fort itself and explore.

✳ ✳ ✳

When a jerk made her open her eyes, she found that the taxi had moved off the NH and was bumping along quite an unknown track. The driver had picked up the man from the *dhaba* and seated him by his left. He was chatting to him like an old crony. It had grown dark outside the windows.

"*Yeh kahan hai? Yeh mujhe kahan laye ho?* (Where is this? Where have you brought me?)" She wanted to scream but there was a cloth tied tightly around her mouth, stinking of hair oil. She realized instantly what was happening. She had once watched too much TV not to. She gripped the driver's hair from the back. The other man sprang up and caught her hands in his grip. The taxi hurtled on, over uneven ground. Her heart began to beat unevenly as well.

When the taxi came to a stop, she saw that it was a wooded spot with no lights nearby. The other man hissed, "*Paise nikal* (Get the money out.)"

She would have, but even before she could, the driver, who knew the money to be there in her *jhola*, took it out himself. She stared, unable to move her limbs which were getting cold and numb.

Hunting further in the side bag, she saw him come upon the ornaments tied up in the scarf. He loosened the knot. The ornaments glinted in the dark. Kushi knew because she saw them reflected in the man's eyes.

"It's all imitation," Kushi wanted to say but couldn't. The man stuffed the ornaments into his pocket and then threw her down upon the car seat.

"*Ab kuchh mazza le*? (Shall we have some fun now?)" he asked the other one.

"*Kiun nahin! Akeli hai* (Why not? She is alone)," he answered.

"*Utni buddhi bhi nahin hai* (Not that old either). *Bas, thodisi pagal lagti hai.* (Just seems a bit mad.)"

"*To kya?* (So, what?)"

Big sweaty hands came to caress her throat, and then her breasts.

For one moment she was terrified but then she went beyond all feelings.

Her heart gave a big thump and just stopped.

A long gurgle came out of her along with some body waste as the muscles relaxed. Evacuation above and below – that's the way life makes its exit.

She made no movement when the driver fell upon her, coming down from the throat and chest, pulling up her *sari* and yanking her thighs wide open. No shrieks came out of her as he rammed again and again into her. Then it was the other one's turn. As even now there was not the slightest protest from her, he looked closely into her face and then laid his oily head upon her dishevelled breasts. "*Arre, yeh to khatam*! (This one is finished!)" he raised his head and whispered in a voice of awe.

"*Kya bakte ho*! *Kaise*! (What nonsense! How!)" the taxi driver seemed equally astounded. He switched on the light above the driver's seat and peered into her face.

The other man gripped her shoulders and shook her. "*Saali to sachmuch mari hai*! (The accursed one is really killed!)" He dropped her and recoiled.

"*Ab kya*? (Now what?)" The taxi driver raised his arm and reached out for the light switch. In the darkness that came back, the two of them lugged her inert body out of the taxi and threw it down on the ground. They denuded her of all her clothes. They rolled them into the *jhola* which held her identification papers and release certificate, and flung the pile away into some bushes. They poured a little petrol over it, struck a match and set it on fire.

The other man said, "*Saali ke upar bhi*? (On this evil one as well?)"

But the driver said, "*Petrol kum pad jaiga. Bhagna bhi to hai.* (We shall fall short of petrol. We have to get away as well.)"

"*Chalo*," said the other one. "*Kapde kagazad jwala diya. Ab koi nei pehchan payega.* (We have burnt up her clothes and papers. Now no one will get to recognize her.)"

Then they got into the taxi and drove away.

※ ※ ※

Kushi realized that she would never reach Neemrana. Or anywhere else. She could not stir, not to speak of getting up and walking away.

What had happened? She couldn't be dead! But it did seem like that. How? Of what? Of rape? But she knew she had died before the rape had taken place. She had not felt it. It was murder and rape rather than rape and murder.

The night air grew turbulent. Kushi, of course, did not even shiver. The contents of the *jhola*, burning at the edges, got a little scattered and splattered.

It began to rain. Big drops fell. Kushi got drenched but felt nothing. The *jhola* and its contents stopped burning.

Kushi had felt neither rape nor rain. She was beyond external stimuli. But she still experienced certain internal thoughts and emotions – from some personal depths – vestiges of the essence encapsulated in her body for so long.

She herself was puzzled. How could this be? Then from somewhere in the dark unknown, fragments of the *Gita* in her grandfather's voice came floating down, orchestrating with the wind and water.

"*Na jayate na mriyate va kadachit.* (It never dies or takes birth)"

Her body may have been killed but not the entire entity. 'Something' was still there – not her brain, not any of her sensory organs. Her dreams and desires? Her pain and grief? Recollections? Aspirations? It could not be the soul – Kushi thought. Souls were beyond all that–weren't they? Then what was this strange ability to still think and feel?

But what *was* she thinking and feeling? All she could feel was a sense of deep disappointment, not anger. Her travels – when she was just beginning them afresh – were over. She would not only be unable to go to Neemrana but also to Delhi, Kolkata, and Rajpur, not to speak of Bangkok. These two men, whom she had never harmed, had put an end to all that. Only for a paltry sum of money and ornaments that were 'imitation gold'? Did they know of her years in prison and release this very day? Did they know what this day meant for her?

Kushi had ample time to think of *Nyaya* or Justice during her life in prison. "*Bhagban ne mere sath nyaya nahin kiya,* (The Lord has not been fair to me)" was a common refrain there. Lying on the forest floor on the way to Neemrana, she too had thought about it. Had it been fair of Rahul to do what he did to her, even if he had not actually managed to divorce her? Had it been fair of Brahman, Bhagwan, Ishwar, God or whoever the Almighty was, to punish him with death, that too, through her? Had it been fair upon Kushi to be shut up in prison for the very opposite of what she had wanted – a happy home? It seemed to be so random, so whimsical.

And then to be killed on the very day she had been freed from prison after serving her sentence in full... how fair was that? She had wanted to work, join some meaningful activity, and make use of her learning experience in prison. She had wanted to travel and see the world – whatever little she could and all alone if it had to be so.

Why cut her off from life just then?

* * *

The burst of rain was over. It was getting to be dawn.

Footsteps were coming. Men were drawing near with bottles filled with water to use in their morning defecation. A plastic bottle falling, spraying water on the ground. Kushi heard a shriek and then feet running away– bringing more.

Soon local people gathered around, and the local police arrived at the 'scene of crime' or the 'place of occurrence', as Kushi knew the relevant terms to be.

A police ambulance arrived as close as it could. Kushi was picked up on a stretcher and loaded onto it. A sheet was thrown over her nakedness. Her travels began again. That was something, Kushi felt.

She was driven to a local hospital in the Alwar district (which is what Kushi realized Neemrana fell under) and pronounced 'dead on arrival' – 'brought dead', again, terms that Kushi knew.

As there was nothing to identify her by, she was taken to the nearest police station which had a *murdaghar* where she was wheeled to the morgue in the basement.

As per medico-legal requirements, she had an autopsy performed on her. The medical personnel agreed, "Six per cent of all deaths in India annually are strangulation deaths. But no, this one is not.

The marks on her neck are light and made after she had stopped breathing." They opened her up and found traces of a sleeping drug, but not enough to kill a person. Rape by more than one person had occurred but *post mortem*. However, there were marks and scratches, as well as a few short, oily hairs in her hands, hands possibly clasped *ante mortem*.

How to explain them? The medical men could not agree on this.

She was stitched up and left on her metal bed in the morgue.

"It's a wonder I am not catching a cold. Perhaps it is just as well. Won't even be able to sneeze if I can't even move."

There was a tag around her right big toe. But she wondered if there would ever be anyone to take her out after the requisite identification and formalities.

In her refrigerated state, Kushi felt like Snow White in the glass coffin where the Seven Dwarfs had placed her. But no prince would ever come to revive her and take her off on a white horse to his turreted castle. Even Neemrana had eluded her.

Her unfulfilled desire to travel was still seeking expression. It seethed within her and came out through her orifices as vapour, forming a cloud which slithered out through the chink below the skylight. It travelled – across Ganga, Yamuna and the South Seas, through childhood and youth, Kolkata, Rajpur, East Delhi, Bangkok and Alwar.

The Reclining Buddha had come to the end of his journey but for Kushi, Nirvana seemed far away.

Kushi's body lay in the morgue for almost three weeks – the maximum time a corpse could be stored there. Then one day the cloud carrying her in spirit felt pierced and shattered. A high wind was making the skylight clatter.

Through it came clashing of steel – cries of agony – of more than one. She did not know what to make of it. Then she heard, someone say, "*Kasam se, hum ne nahin mara. Galad kiya lekin mara nahin.* (We swear we did not kill her. We did her wrong but did not kill her.)"

The voice died away in a sort of rattle.

"*Mati mar gayi thi, aur kya* (We lost our heads – that's all.)," the other voice said before trailing away.

Who were these two and why were their voices making it through to her?

Then it struck her. It was the taxi driver and the friend he had picked up. They had died in some sort of an accident and were confessing their sin but dying halfway through. Oh, was this divine justice! To kill off the two men who had 'killed' her? She did not think so.

Now they would never be caught, tried, and brought to trial. What is more, they would be of no help in her identification. Even if they had destroyed her papers and had no idea of her otherwise, if caught, the driver could at least be made to say where he had picked her up from. That could at least have tracked her back to Delhi.

Now she would have to remain lying here as a *bewaris laash* or unidentified body as long as it was allowed. Then she would be burnt up like garbage.

Secondly, did the men really deserve the death penalty at the hands of the Almighty? Hadn't Kushi always had a weak heart, the reason why as a child she was never encouraged in strenuous sports or dancing? She knew she had been killed by her own fearful heart.

But why did she have such a weak heart? Was *that* fair?

The cloud that was Kushi became dense and coiled up like an Anaconda trying to swallow itself.

✳ ✳ ✳

Someone was calling her. A voice she had once known. A child's voice, changed since puberty. Kuto?

"Mamma!"

The coil of vapour stood poised above Kushi's bed. Kuto was calling for her. She had to be there for him to find her.

There were sounds of the morgue door opening. A policewoman was coming in with two attendants, along with – *Arre*, it was Veena by her side! Thinner and more severe-looking than ever.

But who was this with her? Rahul? But how could that be! So, this was Kuto – grown up to be the living image of his father.

Veena must have called him over from the U.S. to look for her, identify and claim her body, and then perform her last rites. But how had Veena found her? How had she even found out that Kushi was dead?

Veena had her hand clamped over her lips – Kushi knew it was not to let even a cry escape. Kuto looked at her with more curiosity than recognition. He had never seen Kushi after the Bangkok days. Kushi saw Veena request the attendants to give the body a clean-up and put some new clothes on it. She had brought them with her in anticipation. She passed them to the attendants along with a couple of rupee notes, and went out. She and Kuto stood under the tree whose grassy trunk had been visible through the skylight. From the basement, she could see their *salwar-kameez* and jeans.

The attendants were taking off the loose cover on her. They were cleaning her up of the tiny dust particles on her that had almost formed icicles in the cold of the room. They were sprinkling her with more of the disinfectant or sanitizer her body had been preserved in.

The policewoman watching over the 'body' being handed over to the 'family' threw out bits of information to them.

"Rape-and-murder victim. Unidentified till now."

"*Accha! Aur boliye*, Madam*ji*."

"Had herself been in jail for murder. Her *jhola* gave it away."

So, her *jhola* had been found! But hadn't it been burnt?

"That madam – that one outside with the son – had lodged a missing person complaint with the Delhi Police and a photo in the papers. Announced a reward as well."

"Good old Veena, to do all this for me!" said Kushi soundlessly.

The attendants dressed her in fresh clothes. It was refreshing to be in proper clothes again – shrouds though they would become.

The attendants were going with their task while the policewoman was continuing.

"An auto driver from Delhi recognized the picture and said that he had brought her from Tihar half across Delhi. The Delhi police kept watch over the area. They came upon a case of a drunken taxi-walla from Kapashera and his friend – crashing into a truck. They lived for a few days, mumbling in their semi-consciousness about a killing they had done on their way to Neemrana—"

"Hand me that piece of clothing," said one of the hospital attendants to the other.

"Here it is, but Madam *ji*, go on!"

"*Aur kya*! The Delhi Police got in touch with the Rajasthan Police. The dying men had told them roughly where in Alwar they had robbed and raped their victim. From there it was not too difficult for the police to track the hospital where the woman had been 'brought dead' on that day."

"But how did anyone get to know who she was?"

"The police checked the scene of the crime and found half-burnt papers and a sidebag made in Tihar Jail. The killers had thrown them away and set them afire. But that very night there had been rain."

"*Kya baathai!* (Astonishing!) They lay there all this while!"

"Well, it was a deserted place. Hardly anyone went there."

"But why was she killed? *Chori?* (Theft?)"

"The taxi-walla said that she was carrying cash and jewellery that he took to be of gold. She was travelling alone and seemed kind of dull. Didn't know where she was going. Maybe a nut case…An idea had come to him as he drove on. He had called up a friend on his mobile phone and asked him to be there in a *dhaba* ahead. There he had drugged her tea with sleeping pills he sometimes used himself. Then as she had dozed off, they had reached a deserted spot they were familiar with where the two of them had set upon her. But they denied the killing and admitted only to the rape– even when they were giving their deathbed confessions to the police."

"Yes, yes. That's right," Kushi eagerly put in. But, of course, nobody could hear her.

"Could be the truth, you know. She was weak – just out of jail as her papers showed through their burns. The sleeping drug and the shock could have been enough to kill. The rape took place after that."

"We are all women – we in our uniform and she in these shrouds. *Chalo*! I think she is done," said one of the hospital attendants. The other nodded. "Okay," said the policemen.

Another man – probably a doctor – came in with some papers. Veena and Kuto came in. It was Kuto who did the signing. Then 'the body' was handed over to them.

∗ ∗ ∗

Kushi was put into a black hearse that was waiting there by Veena's arrangement. She was placed on a bamboo lattice or framework covered with flowers and garlands. In the air-conditioned vehicle, Veena and Kuto each held one of her cold hands as the driver started.

"If only I had not been away at that stupid international conference! If only that lawyer had not got you that 'good conduct' thing! If only you had sensibly checked into a hotel and waited for me to come back! Why go off into Alwar? Oh, I am so cross."

"I just wanted to D.I.Y.," Kushi wanted to say meekly. "More travels?" she wondered as the hearse drove her back to Delhi and through it.

Veena was speaking to someone. "Yes, we have got her. But have you all reached? Yes. Just wait at the gate." To someone at the other end, she added, "I need you to be there, and hold me if I break down."

That someone said something, and Veena replied, "I have been strong all these years only because you were there –messaging, meeting and mentoring me."

Now, who was this? Who had Veena hitched up with at long last?

Veena was going on, "Yes, it's Kushi who has brought us together!"

Kuto was now bending over her forehead. His long locks were almost touching her face. Ah, smelling of foreign lands, just like Rahul.

"Forgive me for taking Daddy away from you. Believe me that I did not do it on purpose. It was my love, not hatred, that killed him. It was my passion for him, not anger that flung him against the wall. But will you understand?"

14

DELHI AGAIN

*T*he hearse reached from Alwar to Delhi and made its way through to the Lodi Road Crematorium. Kushi was unloaded from the hearse and at once caught sight of Tapen and Papu. Tapen, grey-haired and bespectacled, came forward and touched Kushi's hair in a gesture of affection. Immediately Veena caught hold of him and collapsed into his arms in noisy tears. A dam had burst.

So, it was Tapen, of all persons, that Veena had been talking to! But when did it start? How did it grow? Exchanging reports about the contaminated fields of Rajpur? Discussing Kushi as she went from Bangkok to Tihar and then into the unknown?

This was something she realized she would never know.

The vaporous cloud hanging about Kushi began to shed all its load. If spirits could cry, Kushi did. Glad tears or sad? She herself did not know. She had not lost either Tapen or Veena. But there had been some feeling in her that Tapen was hers, hers alone. That trust – or possessiveness – was gone as she saw Tapen holding Veena as she had asked him to.

"Keep your hands off each other!" She wanted to shout, but obviously, couldn't. This was her last connection with earthly feelings – envy or even a sense of betrayal. Then it was gone as she reminded herself that it was her memory that they were holding in their embrace. Perhaps they would do so, every time they embraced. It was her last chance of enjoying by relinquishing, *tena tena tyaktena bhunjithah.*

There were a few sudden drops from the sky and a gust of wind as if to remind everyone of the work at hand.

With Tapen steadying Veena, and Kuto looking around dazed, it was Papu who made inquiries at the crematorium office where superwoman Veena had booked a slot for Kushi. Again, there were papers to be signed and a standard application to be made for the ashes and leftover bones to be preserved for later immersion in holy waters.

Kushi, on her bamboo framework, was taken to the crematorium. It had a chimneyed furnace with a tray jutting out at floor level.

Kushi was lowered onto the tray.

A priest appeared from somewhere and chanted the name of Hari over her. He lit some incense sticks and sprinkled some water on her. Then the tray was pushed in and Kuto began to cry the way he used to as a kid.

But Kushi saw the electric fire glow red and yellow at her head. Elation! She was in for some more travel!

Hours later, the workers in the crematorium took out the ashes and parts that had not quite burnt away. They put them in a container with a red cloth tied to its mouth, labelled it and kept it in their office. There were a number of such packets there. Kushi found out that this was the procedure for everybody cremated here. The remains were collected a while later and given out to family members who came with a slip or receipt given out at cremation.

Veena returned in two days, with Kuto, Tapen and Papu. They had a pretty earthenware container patterned with slits and holes. The handiwork of some potter, sold perhaps in Dilli Haat.

Into it, Kushi's remains were put.

They got into a cab. Kushi gathered that they had hired it for Garh-Ganga in Garh-Mukteshwar, Hapur.

"Hardwar would perhaps be better," said Veena, "but many do go to this Mini-Hardwar."

It was an ancient place, Kushi knew, possibly part of Hastinapura, the Kaurava capital, and mentioned in the *Mahabharata* and the *Bhagavata Purana*.

Yamuna would have been enough for me, Kushi thought. She had spent so many years at Jamnapar, built up her family there and destroyed it too. She was in no particular need of Ganga-*prapti*. But she could not tell them so. Besides, why give up the chance of a bit more travel – one last bit?

The cab sped past Meerut, the Hastinapur Reserve Forest, and roadside restaurants and outlets selling mats, stools and other local craftware. They made a bright, moving picture. From the windows, Kushi saw the cab make a stop and Tapen and Papu get a taste of the local jaggery.

"Just like at Rajpur," they said and thrust a piece into Kuto's mouth.

15

EPILOGUE – FROM THE BED OF WATER

*F*inally, there was the spread of the Ganga before them with the mid-day sun upon it. The river had somewhat changed course since the *Mahabharata* times when the ashes of the Kauravas had been immersed in her waters. But the longstanding faith of people had not.

Veena handed the container over to Kuto and got down. Through its holes and slits, Kushi glimpsed temple tops, a clock tower, and stalls selling flowery offerings. Then Papu and Kuto – brother and son – got on to a small boat with the priest and the boatman. On either side, there were people taking dips while boats like theirs were rowing further towards the middle of the river which was deeper and considered better for the immersion of ashes.

The priest muttered his chants.

Epilogue – From the Bed of Water

But Kushi herself asked the Brahman to help her further on her travels. '*Gamaya*' – make me go – that was the most repeated word in the *shloka –Asato ma sadgamaya, Tamaso ma jyotirgamaya, Mrityorma amritam gamaya*. She was excited that she was going to a new world – steady, bright and blissful.

But she was a bit nervous as well – just as she had been while going to school. She added a prayer of her own– the little prayer she had made up long ago and never forgotten.

All the sums will come out right, won't they?

I have taken everything along, haven't I?

I won't pee or poop at school, will I?

My panty won't come open, will it?

The sums had all gone wrong. She had not taken anything along. Wherever she was going, she would be incontinent and exposed before the Creator – whoever He was. But this was the only prayer – *her* prayer –and she had to say it as she went away from the world that had been her home for so long. Her *preta* days would be over, thought Kushi, her tossing and turning, her going to and fro. On the bed of water, she would float – reach her journey's end, perhaps meeting Rahul there.

Kuto bent over one side of the boat and floated the ashes into the water. They spread across in widening ripples and whorls. Sun, sky, people, boat and floating flowers added colour to them. Kushi began to draw the water pictures that as a child she had loved to draw on the floor.

www.ingramcontent.com/pod-product-compliance
Lightning Source LLC
LaVergne TN
LVHW041705070526
838199LV00045B/1210